The **Awesome**
Diary of
Charlie Bottle
- The Donut Hole Truth of My Awesome Christmas

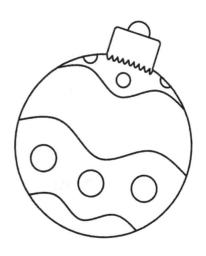

HELLO, welcome to my awesome diary. I'm Charlie Bottle...

This is my mum...

This is my little sister...

This is my Best Friend, Elz ...

I could let you believe that I started this diary on the first of January but if I told you that, then well...

1. I would be telling a HUGE HAIRY fib

Hairy Fib

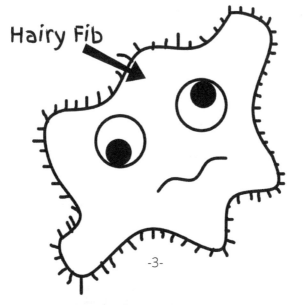

AND...

2. If I had started in January, then you would never get to read about all the exciting stuff that has happened over Christmas. I'm talking MEGA exciting, GROOVYRIFFIC, out of this world SUPERTASTIC! I am going to squeal SO LOUD like a dog's squeaky toy because that is how excited I am.

SQUEEEAAKKK!!

You are probably thinking 'If it's a diary Charlie, how can you start it before January?' Ok, SMARTY-PANTS, I understand the way you think, but MY mum said I could start my diary any time I like because it's really just a notebook. So, I started my all new AMAZING, MUST read diary on the first day of December. This was when Christmas began in our house. It's when SUPER SECRET and MAGICAL things, that were going to happen, were getting even closer. The kind of things you will NEVER believe! It's okay though, because I know it's true and that's all that matters. But if you are SUPER AWESOME like me, you will know that what I'm about to open your eyes to, is the truth, the donut hole truth and nothing but the truth, so help me christmas baubles!

The
Awesome Diary
Of
Charlie Bottle

Are you sitting comfortably? If you are a grown-up reading this, please take note of all the knowledge I am kindly sharing with you in my diary. I feel that this may be of some use to you in the future OR, if you are a kid like me, then I feel it is your duty to pass on your newfound knowledge onto the grown-ups in your life. Believe me, they will thank you for this because I heard that when you get older you lose brain cells. I often wondered what those white bits were on some grown-up shoulders. Mum says it's dandruff but I'm not convinced...

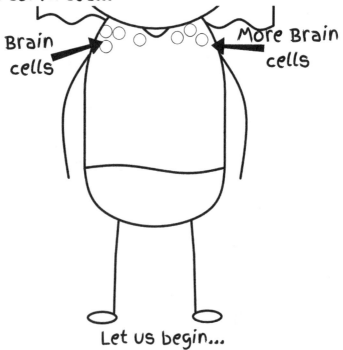

Let us begin...

CHRISTMAS RULEZ

Christmas Day has to be the BEST. DAY. EVER. There are the presents, the decorations, the food, the colourful lights AND we get to celebrate it EVERY, single year! Honestly though why do they have to put so many days in between?? 365 days to be precise! But seriously, that's like FOREVER! I reckon there was a man named President BARMY BRAINS who made that rule up.

PRESIDENT
BARMY BRAINS
THE FIRST

Christmas should be at least once a week! What better way to spend the weekend is there? I mean I wouldn't mind celebrating my birthday every week, so I don't think Jesus would mind either. In fact, I think he would LOVE it. When I explain this to Mum, she says she would never be able to afford it. She said that buying presents every week would be expensive. She even said it would be boring if we did. HAHA! LOLZ! Grown-ups can be SO funny. There's no way Christmas once a week would be boring. I did tell her I wouldn't mind not having presents every time but she insists it's just an ANN-YULE thing, I don't know who Ann is but I definitely know what the Yule part is for...Chocolate YULE logs. They are one of the tastiest things ever. Soft and swirly cake covered in chocolate fudge icing...Mmmmmm SQUEALICIOUS!

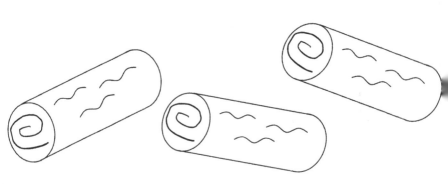

ANN (who is she?)

+

YULE (log)

Second best pudding is trifle. It's that wibbly-wobbly jelly and custard with LASHINGS OF CREAM. Mum tried putting fruit in the jelly a few years ago. EWWW! The HORROR! It was DISGUSTING! It took all the wibble and wobble out of it. Trifle had been in first place until that happened BUT now Chocolate Yule Log has taken over just in case Mum gets any funny ideas again! As for Christmas pudding?... BLEURRGH!

I don't know who invented it, but I feel that we may need to have words about such child cruelty in food form! NO amount of custard is going to make THAT taste any better!

Nope!
Still yucky!
100% GROSS
Positively BIG GRANNY PANTS!

I wouldn't even be surprised if they were serving time in jail for creating such evilness alongside the Sprout-Man and the Aubergine-lady.

FIRST DAY OF DECEMBER

Today is the first day of December, which means we get to open our chocolate advent calendars. Mum chose mine this year. Mum is ACE at choosing. Sometimes I think she knows me better than I do. She got me a MarshyMelts SuperDuper, CHOCCYRIFFIC advent calendar... MY FAVOURITE! Behind each door is a small MarshyMelts chocolate BUT on the last day, I will get a HUGE bar of it, ALL TO MYSELF! Another reason Christmas is so EPIC.

HUGE BAR OF CHOCOLATE
(All for Me - yum!)

My little sister, Melly (short for Melody), got a MarshyMelts ChoccyButton one. She's only a baby and only has one tooth at the front so, it's safer for her to eat those. As far as little sisters go, she's cute! I think she loves MarshyMelts almost as much as I do. However, she spreads most of her chocolate over her face which is a little bit gross. It's a total waste of chocolate too!

Chocolate

Mum said I used to do the same. She even said she has photos of me like it. I refuse to see those, and continue to live as forever-perfect in my imagination.

Very Shiny Halo

Not only is it the first day of December but it's also Saturday, and that means NO SCHOOL!! Mum took me and Melly Christmas shopping in town. We waited until the late afternoon when they had put on the Christmas lights. It looked SO magical. Seeing the town like that makes me feel REALLY happy and gives me a squiggly feeling of excitement in my belly.

Melly 'oohed' and pointed at every single light until a man dressed as Santa said hello to her. I don't think she liked him very much as her bottom lip dropped and she cried. TBH, I don't blame her. We all know that the real Santa hasn't got time to be wandering around our town at this time of year. He's too busy at the North Pole getting ready for Christmas Eve. This Santa wannabe didn't even try to look like the real deal with his long, scruffy grey beard. It drooped from elastic tied around his chin and was so long, it touched his knees! His suit was covered in splodges of mustard from, what I imagine was, his sandwich at lunchtime. A pungent odour of onions wafted from under his arms. It could have been from the very same sandwich! I did ask Mum, but she said I shouldn't ask things like that when we were so close to him, and she made me walk a little faster with her until we got to the next shop. Mental note to self ... 'Don't ask about smells when so close to the person they appear to be steaming off'.

FAKE - SANTA

Mum bought us battered sausage and chips on the way home, but not just your usual variety of battered sausage and chips because we went to the special chip shop on the corner of our road. As well as the usual food you might find in a chip shop, it also sells vegetarian food. Mum said she got us a 'battered vegetarian' sausage. When I told Mum I thought it was a bit cruel, battering a vegetarian, she laughed and said, "Oh Charlie, it's not made from battered vegetarians, it's a vegetarian sausage that has been battered." Personally, I don't see the difference but she said it's a healthier option and I've eaten one before. I have to admit, it tasted yummy so another note to self... 'Vegetarians taste much better than meat'.

Battered Vegetarian Sausage

While we were in the town, I bought Mum a box of MarshyMelts Christmas Creams for Christmas. I found them in a little shop we went into. I've hidden them under some clothes, in the bottom of my wardrobe, so she can't peek.

Do you know how hard it is to actually try and sleep knowing you have the tastiest chocolates just sitting at the bottom of your wardrobe, waiting to be eaten? Do you? Well on a scale of 1 to 10 it's about 150 and it is taking all my goodness superpower to not even open the box. It's so bad, I have to hide under my blanket just to stop the rays of temptation from attacking me. I think the only way is for me to sleep. Night guys!

THE CAT-PAT

DISASTER!! This morning when I woke up, I was led to believe that those MarshyMelts Christmas Creams took over my brain and turned me into a Chocolate munching zombie because my wardrobe was open and so was the box of chocolates.

But on closer inspection, using my AWESOME detective skills, I noticed there were claw marks that can only belong to one *fluffy, grey, ADORABLE* cat who we call Tommy!

Sneaky Cat Scratches

Tommy is part of our family. He is a cute, chunky, super *fluffy* cat and my BEST furry friend...BTW, I said best FURRY friend so, Elz is still my best friend from school. Tommy has *lived with us since I* was two and he always knows when I need him. For example, if I'm feeling sad he will come over to sit with me and keep me company to make me *feel* better.

Tommy

Ok, getting back to the claw marks on the box and the one and only, criminal minded, super cat called Tommy, my suspicions were confirmed when I heard my mum yell "Ewww...Tommy!" followed by the silent, but deadly, trickle of gas that seemed to enter my room and waft, unexpectedly, right up both of my nostrils. I pinched my nose to block any further stench that was heading my way and, very bravely, stepped out to be greeted with the sight of what I like to call a 'CAT-PAT'.

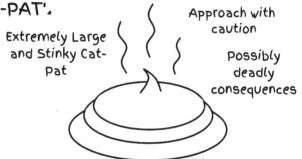

Extremely Large and Stinky Cat-Pat

Approach with caution

Possibly deadly consequences

Of course I couldn't tell Mum what had made Tommy do that STINKERIFFIC poo because then I would have to tell her that I had bought her some chocolates for christmas. Luckily, Tommy hadn't eaten all of them so, there were some left. My nan and grandad always say "waste not want not" so I just stepped back into my room and tucked the rest away.

After mum cleaned up Tommy's stinky business, I checked the coast was clear. I didn't want to face any after the crime questioning. I put on my best tired, 'I don't know what happened' face and went downstairs. Thankfully, the green gas odour had been drowned out by the sweet smell of pancakes with Lemon and Sugar. Lemon and sugar is the ONLY way to eat pancakes, so don't let anyone tell you otherwise! Oh, and it appears to be a great air freshener too!... who knew??

Despite the similarity of their shape to the gift that Tommy had left on the carpet this morning, I couldn't resist eating both of my pancakes. To be honest there isn't anything in the WHOLE world that could put me off them.

Best Pancakes Ever

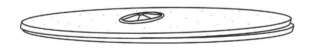

By the time Melly had finished her breakfast she was covered in chocolate topping. She even had it in her hair. I wiped her hands and helped her prize the chocolate button from her advent calendar and I got the chocolate from mine. We both sat for a bliss filled few seconds munching on what can only be described as MarshyMelts TOTAL SCRUMPLETASTIC GENIUS chocolate.

After breakfast, mum said we could put the Christmas tree up. Every year we do this as a team. It's just me, Mum and Melly. I normally put the Star on the tree but this year I told mum that Melly can do it. She is a little bit older and it's only fair to take turns. Mum said she was very proud of me for being so thoughtful.

Sticker

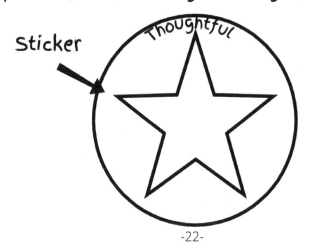

In the end, I did need to help Melly a little bit. She thought that the star was something to eat and kept putting it in her mouth rather than on top of the tree! So now we have made a promise to each other... We promised we will put the star on the tree TOGETHER every year. Well, I think she promised because I am sure the "gurrrrrr, brrrrr" was her way of saying "Yes Charlie, I promise!"

The living room looks so cosy. It's now filled with Christmas lights. They are on the tree and along the shelves and there are lots of sparkly decorations everywhere. Mum said we can put balloons up closer to Christmas day to make it EXTRA special. She said if we did it now, they will all shrink and go 'all droopy' by Christmas. Err not a very christmassy look... am I right?

Talking of 'christmassy', tonight we had our first Christmas hot Chocolate with pink and white, tiny Marshmallows, and cream. Mum said we had earned it after working so hard making the house look all magical. I agree and it was DELICIOUS! Although, it was slightly ruined by that awful swirly tummy I get every Sunday evening. It's because I know that it's school tomorrow. Well, I guess I should get some sleep now as I have to get up early. Night Night!

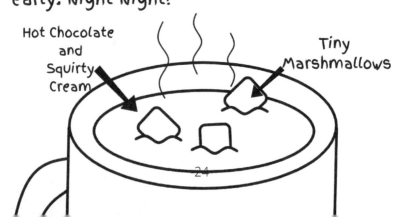

Hot Chocolate and Squirty Cream

Tiny Marshmallows

24

IS IT A MOUSE? IS IT A SPIDER? NO IT'S A ... I HAVE NO IDEA!

When I woke up this morning, it was to the unexpected sight of my mum's bottom sticking out from underneath my bed. When I asked her what she was doing, she told me she heard a scratching noise. She thinks we have a mouse in our house and she was looking for it. The only problem was that she didn't know where it was coming from. I'm not sure it is a mouse though, because Tommy hasn't even noticed it. He looked just as fed up as I was that it was Monday and his sleep had been disturbed. Pfft! I wish I was a cat! If I was, I could stay home ALL day and just sleep. I don't think Tommy realizes just how lucky he really is.

Me as A Cat

As you can tell, I don't like school that much. It's not a secret and I know I'm not the only one that *feels* this way. To be honest, there is ONLY one good thing about it and that's my friend Elz who I mentioned earlier. I think *if* he wasn't there, I would definitely give school a big fat ZERO out of ten! Our teacher Mrs Moody has the PERFECT name because she is DEFINITELY more moody than happy. If there was a pie chart of Mrs Moody's HAPPY days and her MOODY days, with the happy day parts of the pie filled with sweet yummy stuff and her moody day parts filled with mouldy sprouts and rotten aubergines all mixed up, the pie would be TOTALLY gross! There would be far more aubergines and sprouts in that pie than sweet stuff that's for sure!

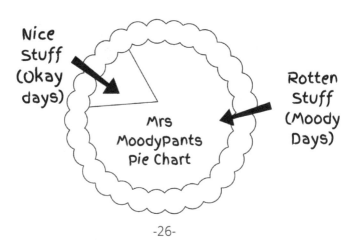

Nice Stuff (Okay days)

Rotten Stuff (Moody Days)

Mrs MoodyPants Pie Chart

Today, Mrs Moody was proper CRANKY! I mean double as moody as her normal moody. She told Elz off for wearing orange trainers. Personally, I thought they looked really COOL. Anyway, why do the days at school ALWAYS feel so much longer when Mrs Moody is like that? I think she's a secret sorceress and casts her dark magic over us just so that we suffer for longer. I wish she wouldn't. Doesn't she know that being in a classroom with a grumpy teacher is horrible? I can't concentrate. I can't even think. Sometimes I worry I'm breathing too loud and will get shouted at for it. If I'm honest, this is why I don't like school.

Mrs Moody

Mrs Moody's very own Storm cloud

Sorry if that was a bit deep... Mum says I should always talk about how I *feel* and this diary is great for just that! It makes me feel a little bit better about the things that worry me.

Having my BEST friend, Elz, with me at school makes it so much easier. We get to have fun at morning and lunch break and we silently support each other in each lesson. Maybe one day I will become a teacher and show them how it's really done. My class will LOVE coming to school. I would give away free MarshyMelts to everyone, EVERY day, just for turning up and every day would be an Art day. I would be the BEST teacher EVER!

At breaktime, me and Elz sat on our usual bench in the playground. BTW, Elz's real name is Elijah but he says he prefers to be called Elz. He doesn't like the playground. He says it's too loud and busy. He worries about being accidentally knocked over so, I sit with him every day. I don't mind though as we sit and play board games that we take to school in our bags or sometimes we draw in our sketch books. On rainy days we go to the library. Our favourite board game is 'Slides and Trampolines' even though I always land on the longest slide in the game and have to start back at the beginning. It's still fun, but today we were RUDELY interrupted by Bully Beatrice AKA BUMFACE.

Bully
Beatrice
aka
BUMFACE

BUMFACE is my name, Being Mean is My game!

WE KNOW!!!

Bully Beatrice thinks she is SO cool, smart and pretty but she's NOT. If she was nice then maybe I would think she was a little bit pretty, but she's just a big MEANIE. She used to bug us every day and I mean EVERY day. Elz used to get really upset BUT we've learned that *if we ignore her, as though she's invisible,* her face goes as red as a baboons bottom (the reason why we call her bumface) and she storms off swishing her ponytail like a horse shaking poo off it's butt.

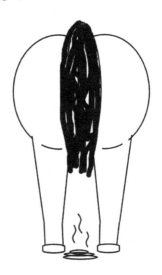

Horse's Butt
for demonstration
purposes (obvs)

She doesn't do it every day anymore, (not the swishy bit but the bullying bit) but sometimes, like today she gets bored and comes over to us just to be nasty. She will have to do better than that to make us break our 'we don't deal with bullies' silence. BEST FRIENDS STICK TOGETHER.

ME → ELZ ←

BEST FRIENDS

In the afternoon, Mrs Moody had to go home. They didn't tell us why but this made me happy. I don't want anything bad to happen to her, obvs, but it was a nice break from the usual tension in our classroom. I actually felt like I could breathe. Instead, we had Mr Potts, our headteacher. He said that, even though it's only the beginning of December we could make Christmas cards. RESULT! I love art and so does Elz. We are going to become famous illustrators when we grow up. Illustrator is a fancy word for people who do drawings in books just like the ones in my diary. What I love the most about it is how you don't have to draw like everyone else. You just neaten up and practice your own drawings which makes you have your own style of illustration. How cool is that?!

I made my card for Santa. I thought it would be nice if I sent him my letter in a card this year. He must get thousands of plain letters so, as he works so hard, I made him a SUPER-DOOPER, SPARKLE-TASTIC card. I hope he likes it.

My Card

HO! HO! HO!

Happy Christmas Santa

I'm not sure what I want to ask Santa for this Christmas. I think I would like to ask him for something for Mum. She looks after me and Melly , goes to work, cleans the house and lots more. She does it all on her own, never moans about it and always with a smile. My mum is AMAZING! I just have to find out if there is anything she would really like. The rest of my class keep talking about the new zSPHERE 5 gaming console. It looks BRILLIANT. There are so many cool games to play and, if I had one, I could play with Elz even if we aren't in the same house! How awesome is that? I know mum could never afford one so I haven't even asked her, and because I really would like a gift for Mum, I won't be asking Santa for one either. This year I want to show Mum just how much me and Melly love her so the zSPHERE5 will just have to wait. All I have to do now is spark up my super detective skills and find out what she really wants. I think I will give Nan and Grandad a call tomorrow to ask if they can help me too.

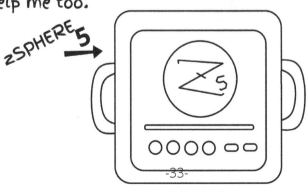

zSPHERE 5

WHAT WAS THAT NOISE?

Mum's right, there is something in our house. A scratching noise kept waking me up last night. I swear (not a rude swear... it's just a saying) I saw a little face staring at me from inside the drawer by my bed. I went to look but, somehow, the next thing I knew, it was morning and I had to get up and get ready for school. I thought it may have been a dream but I also found a little shoeprint on my carpet so I'm really not sure if it was just a dream. It can't be Mum's... and Melly doesn't wear proper shoes yet, not to mention it is REALLY small... Much smaller than Melly's feet! It is literally no bigger than my thumb.

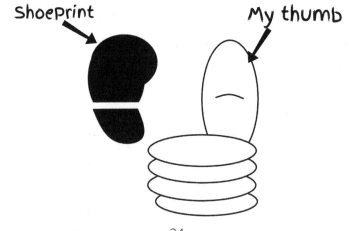

Shoeprint   My thumb

When I got to school this morning, I told Elz all about it. He had a brilliant idea to set up a trap up in my room but only one of those friendly ones. You know the ones that won't hurt it. We just want to know what it is.

Beatrice was sitting behind us, waggling her BIG ears. She listened to every word we said so, at breaktime she thought she would inform us of what she thought about it... SNORRRRRRING!!!

z Z z Z z z Z z Z Z z z Z Z

She told me that I was *fibbing* and that nobody had a foot that small. I said nothing and just remember thinking that it probably matched the size of her brain.

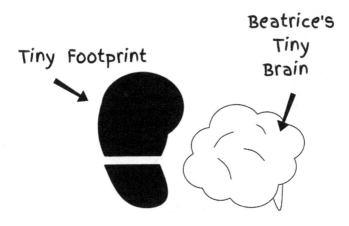

Tiny Footprint

Beatrice's
Tiny
Brain

Mrs Moody wasn't at school today again so we asked Mr Potts if we could stay in at lunchtime to make the trap. Obviously, we didn't tell Mr Potts what we were making. He said that we could, but as long as we were sensible and cleared up any mess that we made. So, at lunchtime, we raided the art cupboard for all the boxes, tape and paper we would need and made this ONE OF A KIND , AMAZING, CREATURE-FRIENDLY TRAP...

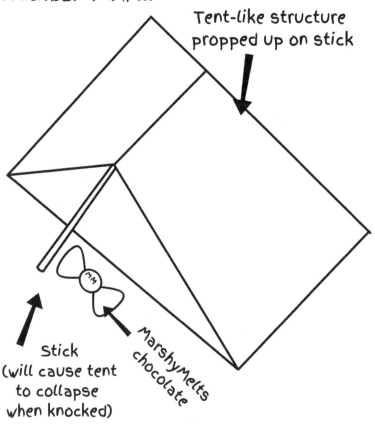

Tent-like structure propped up on stick

Stick
(will cause tent
to collapse
when knocked)

MarshyMelts chocolate

Elz helped me carry it home so it didn't break and so we could get it past bobble-brain Beatrice. She was about to say something horrible to us, as per usual, but stopped suddenly when she saw her dad waiting for her. Then she turned on her SICKLY, goody-goody acting skills. GROSS! She must be a really good actress because all the grown-ups believe her every time. Mrs Moody LOVES her... DOUBLE GROSS!

Mrs MoodyPants!   Bully Beatrice!

YUCK!!

Elz only lives a road away from me so when we said goodbye to each other, I carried it, by myself, the rest of the way. Mum asked me what it was after I had SQUEEEZED it through the door. When I told her, she said it was a good idea and was proud of us that we had made a friendly one, so we didn't hurt the mystery creature.

Because the noise seemed to be coming from my room, Mum agreed that we should set it up in there. I haven't told her about the footprint yet because I don't think she will believe me. I need PROOF and hopefully this trap will give me just that. I've set it up and put one of the MarshyMelts Christmas Creams in it. I mean what (or who) could resist the DELISHISCRUMPTIOUSNESS of those?
Now we just have to wait and see...
Fingers and Toes crossed...

NOTHING OR SOMETHING?

Half way through the week already ... YESSSSS!!! But TRIPLE GROAN, nothing in the trap. They even left the MarshyMelts Christmas Cream!! This leads me to only one possible theory, whatever it is didn't come into my room last night. No-one can resist a MarshyMelts so, it has to be the ONLY explanation.

At breakfast, I asked Mum if she heard anything strange during the night, but she said that she hadn't heard anything. I think this needs some serious discussion with Elz. Anyway, gotta go or I'm going to be late for school. Will write later. C YA!

BACK AGAIN! Sadly, so was Mrs Moody... in our classroom. Beatrice cranked her fake goodness up a notch while the rest of the class cringed at her acting. But despite her best efforts, Mrs Moody shouted at her because she caught her pulling Ruby's pigtails while we were watching a documentary about the war. Beatrice went her usual bright, frustrated and embarassed red when the whole of the class turned to look at her.

Because Bully Beatrice had made her cry, we asked Ruby if she wanted to sit with us, so she moved her chair next to Elz for the rest of the documentary while Beatrice insisted on scowling at us with a face that looked like a dog's bottom... no change there then!

Mouth like a dog's bottom

At Lunchtime I told Elz about the trap and its epic fail. He suggested putting something different in the trap in case whatever it is, doesn't like chocolate! WHAAAAT?! Who doesn't like Chocolate?

Putting aside my absolute shock at such a suggestion, we gave it some serious thought as to what else we could use to trick this mysterious little creature into our AWESOME, new trap. We decided that we will use Gingerbread. I mean it is Christmas and I don't think I know anyone that doesn't love a Gingerbread man. So, on the way home today we popped into Mr Dough's bakery and bought three of them. Clearly there was only one for the trap and the other two were for me and Elz to test. We had to make sure that they met our very specific, awesome trap standards. Which they do. It's a hard job but someone has to do it. LOLZ! So tonight, I have placed a gingerbread man in the trap, ready and waiting. I have also added some jingly bells so I will be able to hear any movement the trap makes when it closes. Got to admit, I am a bit nervous about what it could be, but I am going to be brave.

GULP! I have just woken up to the sound of the trap's jingly bells!!!!! I am just writing this to help me stay calm. Breathe Charlie, just breathe. I am not sure how I am going to do this. What if it's a HUMUNGOUS hairy spider? I really, REALLY don't like spiders. I wouldn't hurt one, but I don't want to find one either. I can't hear any noises coming from the trap, so I don't think it is a GIANT spider, unless of course it has slippers on and that's why I can't hear it?

Cute(ish) Spider

Extra Fluffy Slippers

Maybe I should wake mum up?? ... Nope, I have to do this on my own. I CAN DO THIS! Here I go, wish me luck!

Well, that was a relief, no hairy spider or even a bald one. In fact, there wasn't anything there at all! Well, when I say anything, that's not including the note I found. Mum came in when I was checking the trap, so I hid the note just in case it was top secret. There was no harm in waiting just to read it and if it had been anything weird like a letter from a strange grown-up, I would tell her because, of course, we all know what stranger danger is and how important it is to tell our mum's if we get anything like that, don't we?

I tucked the note under my pillow and showed mum that the gingerbread was missing. She gave me that "Did you eat it Charlie?" look, to which I responded with my best "No I didn't Mother!" raised eyebrows. Mum followed it with even higher, and somewhat scary, raised eyebrows and her "Don't be cheeky, Charlie" face. To which I lowered my eyes to stare at my fidgeting feet and mumbled a quick "sorry mum".

What I've come to realize is that most grown-ups lose their belief in magic as they get older. My mum hasn't lost all of hers yet because she still believes in Santa and the tooth fairy BUT when it comes to the little mysteries in life, they all seem to be shadowed by a gloomy, THUNDEROUS cloud that hovers over them. For this reason, I have decided to stay as young as possible for as long as I can because that cloud seems rather sad to be underneath. AND also, for that reason I kept the letter hidden. I decided that the only one I was going to show was Elz. Well, just for now anyway.

When mum left the room, I grabbed my torch from the top drawer, slipped the note out from under my pillow and carefully opened it.

If you want to know what it said have a look at the next page...

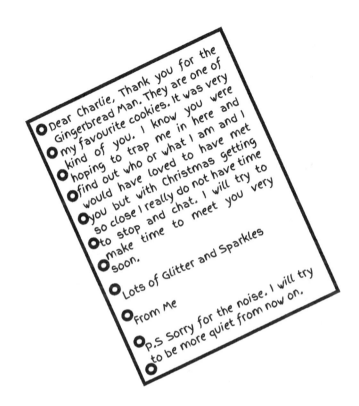

Dear Charlie, Thank you for the Gingerbread Man. They are one of my favourite cookies. It was very kind of you. I know you were hoping to trap me in here and I find out who or what I am and I would have loved to have met you but with Christmas getting so close I really do not have time to stop and chat. I will try to make time to meet you very soon.

Lots of Glitter and Sparkles

From Me

P.S Sorry for the noise. I will try to be more quiet from now on.

Lost for words and very confused, my brain decided that it would fill with all sorts of ideas as to who or what this creature is. I have no name, no photo (not even a drawing) BUT there was something I noticed. They said that they were too busy to stop as we were getting closer to Christmas. Does that mean we have a REAL-LIFE ELF in our house??? EEEEEK!! Imagine that! At first, I thought of Santa but then I remembered the shoe-print I found and there is NO WAY Santa's foot could be smaller than Melly's or as small as my thumb. I have to tell Elz about this at school but for now, somehow, I am going to have to find a way to sleep through the constant thoughts popping about in my head like jumping beans. Maybe those jingly-bells, to wake me up, weren't such a good idea after all. Night guys!

Introducing
Mr Fluff
← - My bear

DO YOU BELIEVE?

I just couldn't sleep with all the questions spinning, like a spinning top, in my mind so I asked mum if she could help. Mum's really into crystals and reiki so she put on some special music for me. This music had the swishing and swooshing sounds of the sea in it. It makes me really sleepy so, eventually, I did fall asleep. Can you imagine how rotten Mrs Moody would be to me if I fell asleep at my desk? I SHUDDER to think! I mean I'm not friends with Bully Beatrice, obvs, but when Mrs Moody shouts, she SHOUTS! I mean like a Super SCARY T-Rex in a very, VERY bad mood! I couldn't help feeling a little bit sorry for Beatrice. I reckon the whole school hears Mrs Moody when she is in full Dragon teacher mode.

Moody
The Dragon
Teacher

After breakfast, I made sure to check that the note was tucked safely in my bag because I wanted to show Elz when I got to school. I didn't walk with him today as his mum took him to the dentist. He came to school with a really cool sticker that the dentist gave him and he bought one for me too. He said that he asked his dentist if he could have one for me and he had said yes. What a cool dentist! Next time I go and have my teeth checked, I will have to ask for a sticker for Elz too. I hope she says yes.

BEST STICKER EVER

At breaktime, I checked the coast was clear and nosey Beatrice wasn't anywhere to be seen. When I was sure it was safe, I showed Elz the note I found in the trap. I asked him what he thought I should do next and he suggested that we get another treat from the bakery on the way home and put it in the trap. He said that maybe, whatever it is, would like that. If I'm really lucky I may get to see what, or who, it is this time, which would be BRILLIANT! But, TBH, only a person with no brain would say no to getting another treat from the bakery anyway so, I didn't need any persuasion.

While we counted down the seconds until school ended (okay we didn't actually count the seconds but it felt that long), we made sure Old MoodyPants couldn't see what we were up to and wrote a list under the desk of all the things we thought the creature could be. Our list so far is this:

o 1. The tooth fairy
o 2. A pixie
o 3. A tiny friendly monster
o 4. A talking mouse
o 5. A lep-re-corn (or however you spell it)
o 6. A magical mini wizard
o 7. A tiny friendly witch
o 8. An elf
o

we know that some of those seem unlikely, but we are really stuck for ideas. I decided to leave the list at school, so mum doesn't see it. I don't want her to ask any awkward questions that I will find too hard to answer.

After dinner, I called Nan and Grandad. I wanted to get some ideas from them about what I should ask Santa to get for mum, this Christmas. They said they didn't really know but that they were sure she would want me to have something for myself. Nan asked me what I would like, I secretly told them about the new zSPHERE 5 and how all my class keep talking about it, but I knew it was too expensive. They said that maybe I should ask Santa for that instead, but I really, REALLY want something for Mum. I will have to continue with my detective skills and find out. I would say that my skills were awesome but even after detective-ing (my new word) I still don't have a clue what mum would like. This has put a HUMUNGOUS doubt over how good my skills really are.

Oops! I forgot to mention that Elz and I bought donuts after school today. We bought three because we had to make sure they were ok, obvs! With the one left over, I added the finishing touches to the trap, ready for tonight. Surely a super sweet cinnamon donut will be enough this time? Fingers, toes and nose crossed. I know!... How can you cross your nose Charlie?? Well, I have no idea but it rhymes so I'm keeping it. HAHA!

CINNAMON DONUTS
MMmmmmmm!

After I placed the donut in the trap, I picked up Tommy and took him downstairs in case he got the clever idea to lick the sugar off the donut. Nobody wants to eat a donut covered in cat dribble. Mum asked if I could look after Melly while she made a phone call. I didn't know that looking after Melly would mean she could call a man about how to get rid of a mouse! That's exactly what Mum is convinced our mystery house visitor is BUT, unless it's a magical one that can write, I am still not so sure. When she finished on the phone she told me all about it but said that they can't come until next week. She said it's because they are *fully* booked...PHEW!! That gives me time to catch this little creature or at least warn them about the man. So, I wrote a letter and placed it under the donut for the creature to find and read. Mum did promise me that the man wouldn't hurt it but I'm not even sure I want it to leave.

Just in case you are wondering what words I wrote in my letter, this is it.....

Not this picture... It's a donut (obvs)

Here it is...

The letter:

Dear friend,

Thank you for leaving me that note last night. I am happy that you liked the gingerbread but also very sorry that I didn't have the chance to meet you. You are probably wondering why I have left a trap out for you, and I hope that it hasn't made you sad or cross. My best friend Elz and I made it, but we wanted to make it a friendly one so that it wouldn't hurt you. Mum has been worried that there is a mouse in my room because we have been hearing a scratching noise. I wasn't sure though as Tommy, my cat, isn't even bothered by the noise. But despite my best detective skills and our list of guesses, Elz and I are still wondering who or what you are.

To say sorry we have left a cinnamon donut for you. Obviously, we had to make sure that they are ok so we had one ourselves and can assure you they are SQUIDGYLICIOUS. If you would like to leave us another letter then that would be great too.

Yours friendly
Charlie

I really hope they leave another letter for us or, even better, I will see them Friday!

FRI-YAY!

Finally, it is FRIDAY or, as me and Elz like to call it, FRI-YAY because this means we have ONLY one more totally BORING, SNOOZE-WORTHY day at school until the weekend. Weekends mean No Mrs Moody and No Beatrice for two whole days!!! However, we still have to try and survive for the next six hours. But today I have something new and totally AWESOME to show Elz!

When I woke up this morning, the trap hadn't moved BUT the donut was gone and so was my letter. We are dealing with a seriously stealthy creature here!

Where the donut and my letter had been, I found something else in their place. It was ANOTHER note. This note told me that the creature I have been trying to catch is ... WAIT FOR IT...Are you sitting down? I really think you need to sit down... Okay, here goes our little friend is ... AN ELF!!!!!!
I KNOW RIGHT?!!

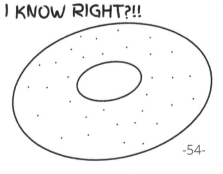

I'm not making this up I swear! ... Right, before I carry on, I need to clear this up... When I say 'I swear' it is just another way of saying 'I promise'. Mum says it's just a phrase so I can use it. I swear to you that it's not a rude swear so I am actually swearing that I'm not swearing... What a brain twister. Lolz.

After thanking me for the yummy donut, he told me that he's Santa's head elf and that he had been sent on a mission to find a child he said was kind and thoughtful enough. Kind and thoughtful enough for what though? I am so confused. I can't believe that's all he wrote. Now I'm left with even more questions. Oh, and he said that there was no need to worry about the man coming next week to catch the imaginary mouse because tonight is his last night here and they will never be able to catch him at the North Pole. Phew!

However, right now, my head is a blur of questions so, there is only one thing I have to do and that is write them all down on paper at breaktime, with my best friend. I have one last chance to get this right or I will be left forever wondering. I wonder if

Elz has any questions he wants to ask? If he has, we will write those down too because he will be just as confused as I am. Must get ready for school now. Will write later with more news!

My Brain being SUPER confused... although clearly much bigger than Beatrice's!

I ate my breakfast, in a hurry, this morning because, for most of it, I had been in slow-mode. All my thoughts had been jumbled up in my head and racing about like a ball from a pinball machine. It was hard for me to concentrate on anything, let alone just getting ready for school! I really didn't want to be late because then I would've been Mrs Moody's next victim! It's bad enough just trying to stay under her radar without being at the centre of it as the target.

Mum asked if I felt ok. She thought that maybe I was coming down with something and needed a day off. Although the thought of not going to school sounded AWESOME, today was not the day for fake *illnesses*. After convincing her I was *fine*, I asked her if Elz could come over after school and have a sleep over because this needed some serious planning and action. Thankfully, I had convinced her that I was totally fine so she said yes.

I was so excited by everything, I hurried down the road to Elz's house. But in all the rush, I failed to see Bumface Beatrice's foot 'casually' sticking out to the side, ready and waiting, for me to trip over. She really is the nastiest person I know!

It was *followed* by a "Ooh, so sorry Charlie, I didn't see YOU there" which dribbled out of her mouth like green, festering slime. Her dad clearly confused this disgusting slime with sugar, because he told her she was good for saying sorry. He didn't ask ME if I was ok! He was too busy hugging her while she gave me her evilest smile, of satisfaction, over his shoulder. A little bit annoyed and upset, but trying not to show that it bothered me, I scrambled out of the bush where I landed and plucked the twigs and leaves from my hair, as well as the ones that had attached themselves to my clothes. I, then, carried on walking to Elz's house.

I couldn't be worrying about needless things like Beatrice when I had much more important stuff to do, like tell my best friend all about the new magical creature in our lives.

When I got to Elz's house, I asked him about the sleepover tonight. His mum said it was okay if he wanted to. Elz said he did which made me really happy and grateful because I know he finds things, like sleepovers, a little scary. I promised his mum that I would look after him and that is what I am doing.

I could not wait until break to tell Elz my news so, I told him on the way to school watching to see his reaction. I could almost see the questions flying around in his brain like mine have been. We read the letter twice like Santa reads his lists. We both decided that we shouldn't show anyone else ESPECIALLY Beatrice. I hid the letter deep at the bottom of my bag until home time.

Coolest
School Bag
EVER

In class, Mrs Moody looked as relieved as we were that it was Friday. She was still her usual grumpy self but not so much of the SHOUTY-PANTS we were used to.

The Curse Of
Mrs MoodyPants

I'm guessing she may have had a sore throat because the tension was still there in that room. The only difference was that, today, she demonstrated her moodiness with random and rapid, sly looks, scowls and thunderous glares that shot across the classroom every few minutes.

This afternoon they seemed to be mainly directed towards Nigel who sits at the back of the classroom. He thinks that if he sits there, Mrs Moody won't see him eating or copying Jenny's work. Just for the record, he was eating snacks, not Jenny's work... he was only copying that! By the looks Mrs Moody zapped him with today, I think he has been totally BUSTED! Cue Monday's classroom seating change. I can just see it now, we will get into class to be told that we can't sit where we are used to, all because of Nigel. Grrr! I am just hoping that Elz and I don't get separated.

When the school bell rang for the end of the day, I checked to make sure that the letter was still at the bottom of my bag. To my relief, although slightly crumpled and soggy from a leaking drink, it was still there.

Elz and I walked to his home so he could get his pjs, toothbrush and some clean clothes for tomorrow. His mum had made us some chocolate chip cookies for after dinner but we all know that the 'after dinner' part is not law so, we decided to test a few on the way back to my house.

Before we opened the front door, we quickly brushed any crumbs of evidence of the cookies from our clothes and rearranged the rest of them in the box so they looked untouched. With our best innocent looks worn across our faces, we opened the door and handed the cookies over to mum in the kitchen and told her they were for 'after dinner'.

Mum said we could have them after our takeaway tonight! We hardly ever have a takeaway and the best part is that we got PIZZA! Not just any pizza though. We got PEPPERONI PIZZA. The pizza of the Gods!

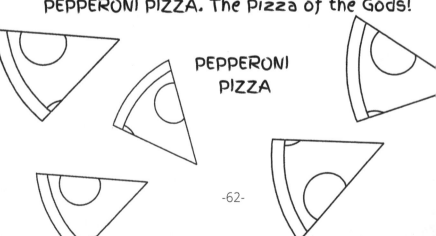

PEPPERONI
PIZZA

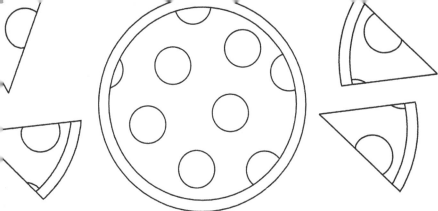

The pizza was so AMAZING, I can't even put it into words! Feeling happy with warm bellies full of the best pizza EVER, Elz and I wrote our list of important questions and created our master plan. One that was simple, yet GENIUS.

We realized that our list really only needs three questions, and they are:

1. Why are you looking for a kind and thoughtful child?
2. Please can we meet you?
3. Are we on the good list?

Now I bet you are wondering what our GENIUS plan is, aren't you? Well, it is very simple...

We PRETEND to be asleep... Genius right?!

We've been practising our snores. They can't be too loud but they have to be just enough to make sure this elf believes that we are GENUINELY sleeping and not pretending AT ALL (obvs). The only problem is that Elz starts laughing after two minutes and then I can't help myself and start laughing too. We just have to make sure that we get this right. It's our last chance!

SATURDAY

Hello again! I have SO much to tell you. I'm not sure whether now is a good time to write it all down but I will give it a go anyway.

First of all, I have to inform you that Elz and I were an EPIC fail at the fake sleeping (note to self, acting will not be my job when I grow up). All of our attempts of fake-sleep achieved only one thing... the giggles. It didn't help when Tommy came in doing all that loving purry stuff that cats do, when he decided to do a HUMUNGOUS bottom blast in Elz's face... Poor Elz. I have never heard Tommy do them that loud before! A tiny squeak now and then maybe but nothing like that! He's not been the same since he ate that MarshyMelts Christmas Cream.

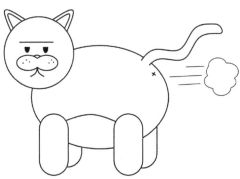

Although that was super funny, let's get to the good bits. Okay so we did end up falling asleep as it got really late with no sign of our elf-friend and we were worn out from all the giggling. We didn't want to go to sleep, it just kind of happened. When I woke up this morning, I felt really disappointed, because I thought I would never know the answers to our questions. I could tell by Elz's face that he was feeling the same too. The trap hadn't been touched and there was no note there, except for our list of questions. We had left a cookie for the elf but that was still there too! I knew that the man who was supposed to catch the 'mouse' hadn't been to our house yet but I did start to panic thinking that maybe Tommy had caught him.

Feeling glum, me and Elz went downstairs to get some breakfast. Mum was making sweet waffles but even that couldn't cheer us up. When mum asked if we were okay, we just said that we were tired. We ate our breakfast and went to the living room to watch some tv. Okay here comes the really cool part...

When we sat down, I noticed something strange. Under the Christmas tree, there was a tiny golden envelope. Too tired to speak, I nudged Elz gently and did that pointy thing you do with your eyes when you don't want to say anything out loud or even move your arms. As Elz looked over, I could tell that he was thinking what I was thinking. Checking that it was just us two, I went over to the tree and picked up the shiny envelope. I could just make out two names on it ...

TO CHARLIE
AND
ELZ

My tummy did that *flip* thing that it does when I'm half nervous and half excited. Feeling the way I did, and because it was fair, I let Elz open the letter. This is what it said:

Dear Charlie and Elijah,

Thank you for leaving that cookie and the letter for me. As you probably know by now, I didn't get time to stop and eat it as tonight I needed to make sure that everything I needed to do was completed. I did see your questions, but I can only answer two of them.... Yes, you can meet me, but not yet and the other is yes you are both on the good lists. Your other question, I can only let you know that you both have been chosen as the kind and thoughtful children. You are probably now wondering why I even came looking for you but that I cannot tell you just yet. I will be returning midday Christmas Eve and although you will not see me, I will leave two very special mince pies for you. You are the only ones that can eat these so please make sure that no-one else eats them, not even a crumb. I will leave them at the bottom of your wardrobe, Charlie. Once you both eat them, you will get all your answers and more.

Happiness and Jingly Bells
Crackerz The Elf

Elz and I stared at each other in shock. Was this really happening? I mean Mince Pies ARE gross, but I think I can eat a magical one from an elf, right? Hopefully magical mince pies from the North Pole taste better than the ones I've tried before.

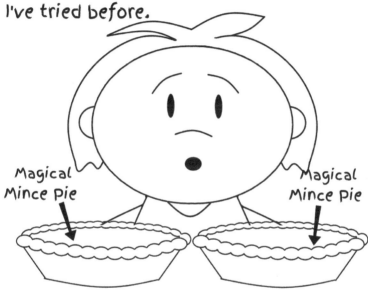

Magical Mince Pie

Magical Mince Pie

Straight away, we started making plans for Christmas eve. Our first thing to do was to call Elz's mum and ask if he could come over on that day. Once we had the all-clear for that, I quickly informed my mum of our plan and ran back out of the room so she couldn't say no... Although, I know she likes Elz and doesn't mind. With that sorted, all we had to do was wait. We have SIXTEEN DAYS to go! I'm not sure I can do this! Send help because the days are going to go MEGA slow and it's going to be SO PAINFUL!!

Elz went home after lunch today because his mum wanted to take him shopping. So, this afternoon, I decided that I would snoop to find out what Mum would like for christmas. It's getting closer now and I need to post my letter to Santa soon. I knew that if I just asked her, she would say that she didn't want anything other than for me and Melly to have a lovely Christmas so, I went into SUPER-SLEUTH mode this time. I listened in on telephone conversations with my radar hearing and that is when I heard mum say "I'd love a new phone but they are so expensive, Becky!" So that is what I asked for in my letter to the big guy... A new phone for Mum. Awesome Detective skills restored!

DETETCTIVE'S
MAGNIFYING
GLASS

I ♡ 🐱

Super Cool
New Phone
For Mum

So, once I knew what to ask Santa for, I sat down to write my letter. I decided it wouldn't be a good idea to write straight on to the card because *if* I did that and made a mistake it would be completely ruined! So, I wrote a letter THEN placed that inside. I didn't have the time to make a mistake and then have to make another card. Santa had to get my letter soon or Mum would never be able to get her present and christmas would be ruined!
Once I was happy with my letter and felt that Santa would be pleased, I folded it and placed it inside the card, then popped both of them into an envelope just the right size. I made sure to doodle lots of

pictures all over the envelope to make Santa happy.

I CANNOT WAIT TO SEE MUM'S FACE WHEN SHE GETS HER NEW PHONE!!! Eeek!!

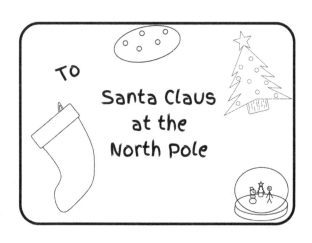

TO

Santa Claus
at the
North Pole

With all the excitement of the last few days and the gloomy reality that there would be no note left for me this morning from our visitor elf, I focused my thoughts on my single MUST-DO thing on my list for today... POST MY LETTER TO SANTA.

   At breakfast, I reminded mum that I needed to go to a postbox. She said that, as we were going food shopping today, we could post it on the way. PERFECT! Then I realized that Melly is too little to write a letter by herself and if she couldn't write a letter then how would Santa know what to give her this Christmas?! In my panic, I ran back upstairs to my room, tore open the original envelope and wrote a little P.S note that said...

"Please can Melly have a Teddy Bear for Christmas (I am writing this for her as she is too little to write to you). Thank You Santa!"

I didn't have time to draw all the doodles on the envelope again so, I just drew a snowman on the front of it instead.

Mum let me post my letter before we went shopping because I was worried I might lose it which would have been a total disaster! So, now, my letter is officially on its way to the North Pole!! YESSS!!!!! Fingers, Toes and Christmas Bows crossed, my mum will get a new phone this Christmas.

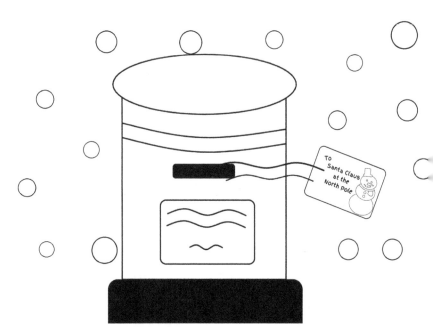

Knowing that my letter was safely on it's way to the North Pole, we headed to the local supermarket. Now shopping can be either 'SERIOUSLY SNOOZE-WORTHY' or, if there are treats involved, it is classed as 'absolutely essential'. Today was an 'absolutely essential' kind of day because we were shopping for Christmas treats. We don't really get that much but what we do get, we love. Mum always says that if we buy only a few sweet treats, rather than lots of them, then she can afford to buy us better presents instead. She says that treats only last a little while, but gifts can last forever, and, even though I love treats, I know she's right because my mum is clever like that.

As Melly is still so little Mum asked me to choose a special sweet treat for both of us. Well, you must know by now which direction I headed in when she said that... That's right! Straight to the MarshyMelts section. I think I could actually hear the angels singing in approval as I floated down the aisle in the glory of all the SCRUMDIDDLYTASTICNESS.

I was on a mission of utter importance...

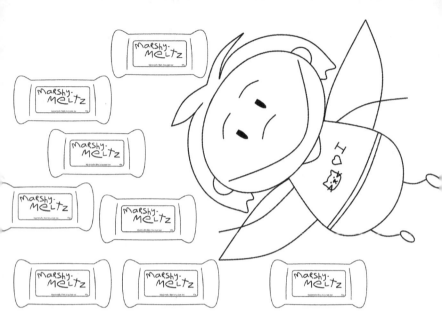

To my absolute horror, I was RUDELY
ripped away from my MARVELLOUS
MarshyMelts daydream by the high-
pitched, torturous, SCREECHING tones of
Beatrice. OF ALL THE DAYS AND TIMES, SHE
HAD TO GO SHOPPING, WHY DID IT HAVE TO
BE WHEN I DID?! I noticed just how much
she sounded like that awful noise of
fingernails scratching down a chalkboard.
If you've never heard that sound, DON'T,
under any circumstances, try it! Your
teeth will never feel the same again... NOT
EVER! Trust me on this! Luckily, she
hadn't seen me and was just SQUAWKING
like a crazy parrot at her mum. I crouched

behind a cardboard Santa to hide. There is NO WAY I was going to let her know I was there!

I hid for a *few* minutes while she and her mum walked past. You should have heard the demands she was squealing at her mum!

I could only imagine my mum's face if I did that... She would ground me for a week! ACTUALLY make that a year! Surely this girl cannot be on Santa's good list?!

My Mum's face if I spoke to her like that...

Feeling like I could breathe again once Beatrice had gone, I chose some MarshyMelts Soft Stars for Melly, MarshMelts ChunkyCrunch for me and a MarshyMelts Christmas Star for my mum. Although Mum would see it, I really wanted to get her something else. I had been feeling a little bad about Tommy's Cat-Pat fiasco and really did need to replace the missing chocolate. (MUM, if you are reading this, I am REALLY sorry, I didn't know that Tommy loves MarshyMelts as much as me, HONEST!)

When we got home, I was determined to make sure that the chocolate was hidden well. So well, in fact, that Tommy wouldn't get his paws on it this time. I did NOT want to suffer the NOSE-MELTING stench like before nor did I want to put my acting skills to the test again because, as we know, they are RUBBISH!

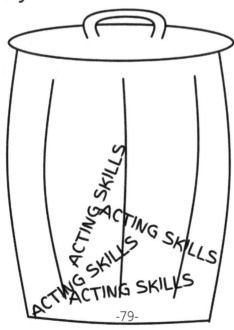

With all that done, it left only time to think about two things...

1. The utter dread of School tomorrow

and

2. Just how long I had to wait until Christmas Eve when our visitor would return.

To try and take my mind off the thought of school and to stop my fidgeting with impatience, I suggested that we all watch a Christmas movie. Mum loved the idea and even cooked some buttery popcorn for us to munchity-crunchity on (BTW, two more new cool words combined) while we watched it. Buttery popcorn is the BEST. I know a lot of people prefer the sweet stuff but for me, the buttery version wins EVERY time, especially when it's just been cooked. YUM-Meeeeeeeeee!

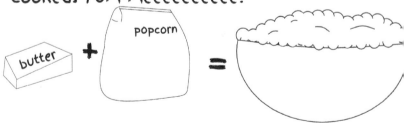

BEST POPCORN EVER

Mum poured the hot, buttery and salty popcorn into a HUGE bowl for us to share. As we sat side by side on the sofa, Melly smeared her special crisps, for babies, all over her face. We closed the curtains and turned out the lights to create our own cinema and watched 'The Magical Elf'. Not the perfect movie to help me forget our very own elf guest or to help calm the impatience bubbling away in my belly, but it did help some of the time pass by quicker.

As you have probably guessed by now, I am in my room and its nearly time for me to sleep. Most Sundays, I would be trying my hardest to stay awake because then Monday would seem like it would take longer to arrive...but this Sunday, as much as I dread school, I don't mind going to sleep. If you're wondering why, then let me tell you... Every sleep I have is one sleep closer to Christmas eve. Not to mention that this is our last week at school before the Christmas holidays...

... RESULT!!!!

First of all, before I begin this week, I need to let you know that I have made the decision not to make this diary thing a daily thing. If you are wondering why, then here is my reason:

I DON'T HAVE ONE...HAHA!

MY diary, MY rules!

All that being said, it is Monday today and this week has had the most amazing start! As you know I was expecting Mrs Moody to be changing where all of us sat in class (because of Nigel) but how happy was I when we were told Mr Potts was going to be teaching us this week? I will tell you ... MEGA HAPPY! It only means that there is no Mrs 'I look like I've been sucking some seriously bitter lemons' Moody crushing our festive spirits, like a GIGANTIC nutcracker, before the holidays.

As each of us sat in our seats the excited chatting began. Nigel lobbed a paper ball at the back of my head but I was not about to let 'The Phantom Nose-Picker' ruin my day so I said nothing. I just turned and glared at him, trying to copy exactly what Mrs Moody does. I think it must have worked because his face dropped and he pointed at Beatrice as though she had done it. I mean I know Beatrice is just as bad as he is but throwing paper balls is really not her style. I also noticed, using my newly restored detective skills that Nigel's hands were covered in NEWSPAPER INK from the paper ball I now had, sitting on my desk, as evidence.

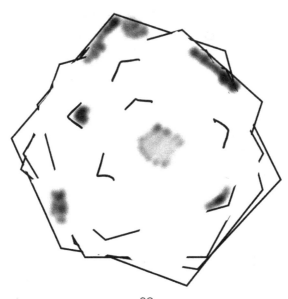

Eventually Mr Potts managed to get us all to be quiet. He told us that Mrs Moody was away for a week and that she would be back after Christmas. Why he needed to tell us that she would be back (which took away some of our excitement)? I have no idea but I'm all for the HERE and NOW and the fact that Mrs Moody is not HERE means I can be happy NOW.

Everyone in our class clearly felt the same as the happy chattering started again and this time it got REALLY loud. The noise got too much for Elz because his ears are a bit sensitive so, Mr Potts said we could go to the 'Quiet room'. I have to admit, the quiet room is one of my favourite places at school. We get to chat to each other without being told off. Today, it was also the perfect place to discuss our expected Christmas Eve visitor.

what I think
Crackers
looks like

Mince Pie

I have to say that I think Elz is just as excited as me, even for sleeping over at mine. You see, we decided that instead of Elz coming over midday on Christmas Eve, he would sleep over on Christmas Eve Eve (BTW, this is the way awesome people refer to the day before Christmas eve).

It's Christmas Eve Eve

Elz said that he had fun at the sleepover last time, so I suggested that we had another one and what better time than Christmas Eve Eve to do just that. I don't think you realize just how amazing it is to hear Elz say he enjoyed the sleepover, and I am super proud of him because I know it hasn't been easy for him like it would be for others.

Despite our excitement for the big event, there is one grim cloud that hangs over us and that cloud is called 'WAITING'. I am no good at it. I get so fidgety and impatient. My nan says that I have 'ants in my pants' and my Grandad says that I'm a 'fidget.........' ummmm! I can't say that word it's a little bit rude but what I can say is that it's another word for bottom that grown-ups use frequently.

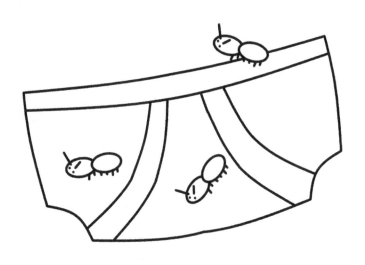

FYI, I DO NOT HAVE ACTUAL ANTS IN MY PANTS! (It's another phrase)

We tried to think of ways to make the days go faster but FAILED miserably! The only thing we can do is try and *fill* our days with as much fun stuff as possible because we all know that fun days *feel* like they go a lot faster than boring days. For example, two days at school feels SO much longer than the two days we get for a weekend. This has to be the work of someone truly evil like Mrs Moody. Maybe time is made by a hamster on one of those wheel thingies they have and as soon as the weekend comes along an evil sorcerer casts a spell on him and he speeds it up AND THEN when it's a school day he makes the poor hamster slow down so we are all in slow-motion. That has to be it, I see no other explanation.

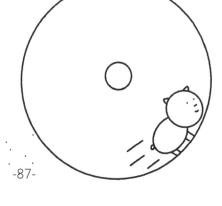

With Mr Potts for our teacher and all the activities he has planned for us at school, I really don't think this week will drag as much as we thought it would. But I don't mind if the evil sorcerer lets the hamster rest because he must get very tired and this week looks like it will be SUPER FUN and Christmassy for us!

CUPCAKES!!!

What a super awesome day! Mr Potts bought in lots of ingredients this morning as well as bowls, spoons, cupcake cases and cooking trays. We got to make our own Christmas cupcakes! He divided us into pairs. Me and Elz stayed together and called ourselves...

chef Charlie

chef Elz

Tm

THE 'CRAZY FOR CUPCAKES' CHEFS

Beatrice moaned when she was paired with Nigel. To be honest, I think he looked more horrified than she did. She told Mr Potts that she couldn't 'POSSIBLY' make cakes with him because he picks his nose (Nigel not Mr Potts!) and she demanded that she was paired with someone else. I think she forgot that Mr Potts wasn't like Mrs Moody because he just told her to stop being mean to Nigel. It is true though, Nigel does pick his nose hence the name 'The Phantom Nose Picker'. I can't go into too much detail because the thought just makes me want to spew, but by the end of the cake making lesson, Beatrice was a dull shade of green and insisted that Nigel took the cakes home with him. She used this moment to gain sucky-up points with Mr Potts and wriggled her way back into his good books.

Grossed out and slightly green Beatrice

Bogey-bun Cake

At lunchtime, we were all allowed to eat one of the cakes we had baked. Me and Elz made vanilla cupcakes with chocolate chips and fudge pieces inside. They were FUDGESCRUMPTIOUS. Elz, being the TOTAL GENIUS that he is, said that we should bake some more cakes for the elf so, we wrote down how to make them. When I got home, I gave the list to mum to see if we had everything we need. Luckily, Mum said she had all the ingredients, and she would save them for us. My mum is TOTALLY AWESOME!!!

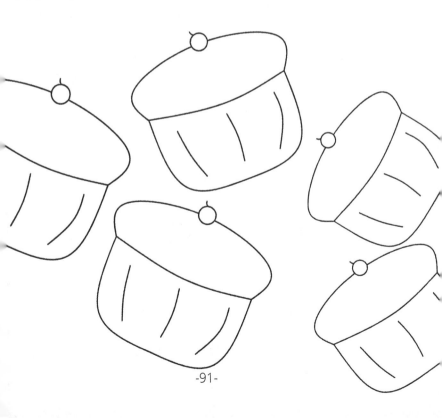

THE TRADITIONAL MOVIE AFTERNOON AT SCHOOL

Today was a bit slow at school. Mr Potts thought it would be 'fun' to watch a movie in the afternoon. We were led to believe we were about to watch an 'epic movie' BUT our hopes unexpectedly and VERY quickly flew out of the window! We stared in despair at a movie what could only have been filmed during the Jurassic era. It had absolutely NO colours except from black, white and grey!! Mr Potts said "it is a classic" and "I used to love this when I was your age". I mean how old is Mr Potts??? I knew he was old but who knew he walked with dinosaurs? I wonder if he had one as a pet? Now that would have been cool.

Mr Pott's Childhood Pet... 'Rex' - Tyrannosaurus Rex

King of The Dinosaurs

I spent most of the movie having an imaginary fight with invisible weights which seemed to be tugging down on my eyelids. They wanted me to sleep, while any energy I had left, trickled out of my toes and disappeared. I know I wasn't the only one because I kept having to nudge Elz to stay awake and at one point I turned around to see Nigel had fallen asleep with his finger wedged up his left nostril... GROSS! Not an image I want to remember or even draw for this diary, THANK YOU VERY MUCH!

The school bell startled most of us back to reality at the very last second of the movie.

Desperate to get out of that classroom, we packed up our bags, dragged our coats on and headed for the school gates. I felt so tired, like someone had replaced my body with a snail's body!

Charlie The Snail

Elz The Snail

The cold air hit us as we stepped into the playground. It was all we needed to revive us. I don't like the cold very much, but I was glad it had saved me from the Jurassic Movie induced state I was in. The only cold that I do like is the one that comes with the snow. I am really hoping it snows this Christmas. We didn't have any last year, it was just rain and sloppy mud everywhere. If it does snow this year, me and Elz have decided that we are going to build the most AMAZING snowman! And if we are really lucky it could lead to a few extra days off school. Fingers, toes and winter clothes crossed, we will have a white christmas.

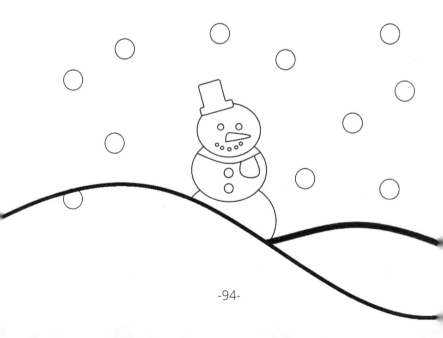

We popped to the bakery on the way home. It's the baker's fault!! We were just casually walking past when we were met with the most delicious smell of hot steaming, just baked, sausage rolls. My tummy growled like I hadn't eaten for weeks!! There was only one thing I could do. It was the kindest thing. I knew I had to feed my dramatic and noisy tummy. I had just enough money to buy one for me and one for Elz.

Sausage Rolls

My mum always taught me that I should always think of others so, even if I only had the money for one, I would have given Elz half of it. It's the kindest thing to do and the right thing to do, too.

After every belly-warming bite had been eaten, I said bye to Elz and walked down the next road back to my home.

This evening, me and Melly, were told to stay in the living room as Mum was wrapping our Christmas presents. Although desperate for a peek, I promised not to look and that I would keep Melly occupied. Not knowing is EXCRUCIATING (my new posh and dramatic word) but I also know that if I did peek, it would take some of the excitement away. After Mum had finished, she handed me a sheet of wrapping paper, the tape and a little box. She said that she had bought a little notebook, like the one I have now. She said it was for Elz, as a gift from me. Now he can create a diary too. We can be diary buddies! How cool is that? I think Elz will love it.

After I gave mum a huge hug, I thanked her, wrapped the diary up in the paper and placed it under our tree to give to Elz on Christmas Eve. I'm even more SUPER-EXCITED now!

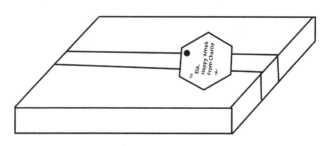

LAST DAY OF SCHOOL BEFORE CHRISTMAS

Well, we made it to the last day at school before the Christmas holidays. As I write this, I can officially say it is over and I am at home with my mum and my little sister. The school closed early at 2 o'clock. They said it was because of 'the weather forecast' but by the looks on most of the teacher's faces, I think it was because they were just as desperate to go home as we were. Apparently, the weatherman said that we were going to have 'heavy snow'. Everyone knows that snow isn't heavy. Can you imagine the news if it was?

"TODAY A MAN WAS CRUSHED BY A FALLING SNOWFLAKE"

NEWS AT SNORE O'CLOCK

This, dear reader, is how I know that the teachers were fibbing!

Despite their desperate attempt to hide the fact that they'd had enough of school, we were all VERY happy to be sent home early. You don't need to convince me to take the afternoon off school!

So here I am about to embark on what, I hope, will be an EPIC Christmas Break filled with adventures that will be even more EPIC!

THE FIRST WEEKEND

The last two days have been what I like to call TOTAL CHILL DAYS. These help me forget all about how much I really don't like school and every little detail of it. If I do these days really well, I may even be lucky enough to forget that it even exists.

Even though it has snowed a lot like the forecast said it would, I would like to take this opportunity to say "I TOLD YOU SO" because as I said earlier the snow was not heavy at all. No-one was crushed by random flying snowflakes and if they had been 'heavy', as we were told, then me and Elz wouldn't have been able to create THE SNOWMAN OF TOTAL AMAZE-SNOWBALL-NESS that is sat outside my living room window.

When it was time to dress our snowman, Mum said she had a drawer of old winter clothes in her bedroom that we could use. When we looked, we couldn't find the usual scarf and hat, but we did find what can only be described as:

1. A bright red hat that had obviously been made especially for a teddy bear because it had two holes at the top. It's a pretty strange thing for my mum to be wearing but maybe she has some hidden teddy bear ears that I don't know about. I'm not saying she has ears like a bear but, you know, like those fancy dress ones you can get for when you *feel* like dressing up as one? That must be *it*.

AND...

2. The strangest and weirdest shape scarf we have ever seen. It is clearly a genius scarf though as there were pockets in it. They look like they may be cup holders as they weren't very deep. What an AWESOME idea!

Although these were quite different to the hat and scarf we were looking for, we were still happy that we'd found our snowman something to wear. We didn't want him to be cold out there on his own. With those bundled in our arms, we hurried out to dress him.

It was getting late when we had finished and we noticed the sun was disappearing quickly. As it was getting darker by the minute, Elz decided to go home before it got too dark and scary for him.

Once Elz had gone, I asked mum if she wanted to have a look at our new frozen friend but because the sky was almost black, she said she would look tomorrow. It makes sense really as she will be able to see him much better during the day time. I can't wait to show her. I think she's going to love him.

TOTALLY EPIC SNOWMAN

Sorry! ... I can't show you before I show mum. It would ruin the surprise.

Monday! Somehow the holidays *feel* more official when it's a weekday and you're not being woken up early to get ready for school. Mum is always up bright and early with Melly so, I never sleep in late anyway but the rush and the panic isn't there. It's such a relief. I quite like the mornings. I don't normally wake up later than 8 o'clock because, as crazy as this may sound, if I do, I *feel* like I've missed the best part of the day.

This morning after breakfast, I was excited to show mum mine and Elz's snowman outside. Even though I was desperate for her to see him, she said she would have a look when we leave the house as we had to go out again today. So, after mum had washed the breakfast dishes, we all bundled into our warm hats, coats, gloves and scarves and trampled out into the cold. Mum wasn't wearing one of her 'teddy bear' hat range. She probably didn't want to wear the ears so, there was no need to wear one. In fact, I don't think I have ever seen her wear her teddy bear ones. If I had teddy bear hats and cool teddy bear ears, I would wear them every day!

Cool Teddy Bear Ear

Cool Teddy Bear Ear

Hat with holes for ears

I ♡ 🐱

As we stepped out of the door, Mrs Parker, from over the road, stopped in front of our house, harrumphed (such an awesome word) REALLY loudly and gave my mum a look of disgust followed by a chorus of REALLY loud 'tutting'. My nan says "If you keep tutting like that, you'll end up blowing your front teeth out!" but, luckily for Mrs Parker, her teeth seemed to be holding on for dear life!

Mum looked as confused, by the tutting, as I was. She, then, gazed in the direction of where Mrs Parker had been staring and her face went TOTALLY white. Her cheeks lit up like two pink, round bulbs. When I asked her if she was ok, the only noises she was making were these strange squeaking ones. I started patting her back trying to burp her like she does to Melly but it didn't help at all. Baffled by her reaction and why my snowman would have given her wind, I could only think it was a result of the TOTAL AWE she was in at how EPIC it was.

Hole for Teddy Bear Ears

HAT

Hole for Teddy Bear Ears

Scarf
Cup holder 1
Cup holder 2

I'm not sure why Mrs Parker looked like she did but I do have two theories...

1. A SERIOUSLY uncomfortable wedgie. You know like the ones that always happen at the most awkward times and you can't do anything about them until there's no-one around to see you remove said wedgie from between cheeks? OR...

2. Maybe she was on one of those 'health kicks' adults talk about and had a grapefruit for breakfast which left a sour bit of it stuck in her teeth. That could explain the tutting too!

When Mrs Parker had gone, Mum asked me which drawer we got the hat and scarf from. I wasn't sure why, but she seemed to put a bit more oomph into the words 'hat' and 'scarf'. Even though that seemed a little strange, I told her that we got them from the drawer in her bedroom like she had told us we could. She seemed to be having a few issues with her voice this morning because after I had said that, she muttered a rather high pitched "uh-huh". It obviously wasn't painful because a huge mischievous grin spread across her face then she chuckled and let out a loud SNORT as she hurried us into the car.

After all that, we headed off out for the morning. Grown-ups are funny creatures, aren't they? Lolz

It wasn't until we got home that mum explained that me and Elz had accidentally taken clothes from the wrong drawer in her room. OOPS!! She suggested that we use her spare woolly hat and scarf instead. I have to admit that I do think our snowman will be a lot more comfortable in these ones. The other scarf we used was a bit weird and he didn't really have any use for the cupholders either.

Later in the evening, Elz phoned and asked if I wanted to go to a Christmas fayre tomorrow with him and his family. Obvs, I said yes... I CAN'T wait. I've already raided my piggy bank so that I can buy some treats for everyone. I hope I have enough so I can buy some for Mum and Melly too...I think I do. SUPER EXCITED!

CHRISTMAS FAYRE DAY

What an EPIC day!!!! It has to be the best fayre I have ever been to. Well, I haven't been to many of them, but of the *few* I have been to, it is DEFINITELY the best!

Elz's mum drove us to the fayre as it was out of town. Her car is not as big as a van, but not as small as my mum's car either. Elz says it's a 'people carrier'. He says it's a posh way to say that the car carries a lot of people. I'm kind of glad they do have one because Elz's younger sister, Nan and Grandad came with us too. It would have been a bit of a squish if we had been in a smaller car, that's for sure.

smaller car

8UTT SQU15HED

The journey to the fayre was a short one but that suited me and Elz just fine. We were desperate to explore. As we stepped out of the people carrier, we were greeted with THE MOST MAGICAL SIGHT EVER!! This wasn't just a fayre, it was a Winter Wonderland. There were twinkling lights on every stand and dotted over every ride. There were stalls that sold:

Cotton candy,

Sugar cookies,

Ginger bread men

The list is endless.

There were elves and a man dressed as Santa. This santa wasn't like the one that Melly got upset with. This one looked like the REAL DEAL! He looked AMAZING. His beard was all white and fluffy, and actually looked like a real beard! He was dressed in a posh, bright, red velvet suit and shiny black boots. His gloves were made of leather and there were shiny golden buttons on his jacket. This santa obviously took his job very seriously! I give him a fab 9/10 on the Santa scale!

We had arrived early at the Christmas Fayre. We did this to avoid the crowds because of how they make Elz feel. He gets really overwhelmed if there are too many people. For this reason, we were the first at most of the stalls and we were able to go on the rides first too. It, also, meant first pick of the treats and hardly any queueing! RESULT!

First, we played Hook-a-duck. They were only plastic ducks otherwise that would just be mean...

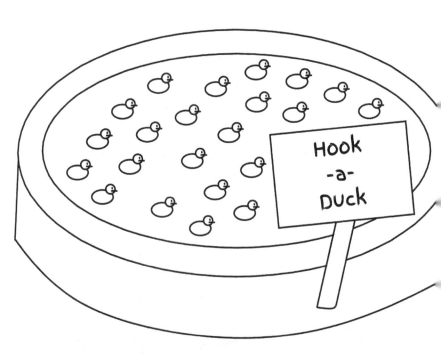

Then, we played hoopla followed by more games!

We went on the bumper cars...

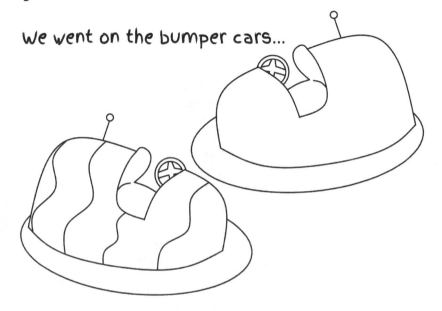

The spinny teacup things...

AND...

The best of all, we went on the Christmas train...

THE CHRISTMASTASTIC TRAIN

The train was my FAVOURITE part. Elz's mum bought us Christmas Cotton Candy that tasted like peppermint and chocolate and I spent my money on some chocolate coins for us all. I was really pleased as I was able to get some to take home for Mum and Melly, too. Today was so much fun!

CHOCKO COINS   CHOCKO COINS

When it started to get very busy, we all bundled back into the car and headed home. I stayed at Elz's house for a little while so, we made a SUPER-COOL snowman for his garden like we did for mine. Now we both have the best gardens in our town.

ELZ'S SUPER-COOL SNOWMAN →

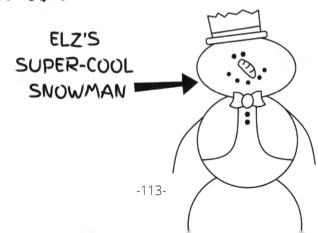

When I got home I told mum all about our day as I shared the chocolate coins out. They weren't MarshyMelts but they were still scrummy. I told Mum all about the rides and how magical the fayre was. Melly chomped on her chocolate coins for what seemed like ages rather than her usual super speedy 'spreading over her face' ritual. Mum said she was chomping slowly on them because she is teething and it makes babies *feel* better when they do that. Teething is when a baby's teeth are growing through their gums. Poor Melly, I feel so sorry for her. Mum says it can be really uncomfortable, sometimes painful and make babies cry. Hopefully those chocolate coins did help Melly. She certainly looked happier after eating them.

Since the Fayre, me and mum have been preparing for Christmas by baking those SPEW-DICULOUS Mince Pies that grown-ups always insist on making. I know I'm going to have to be REALLY brave on Christmas Eve if I have to eat the one the elf said he would leave for me. I don't even think the nose-pinching routine is going to help. You see, it's not the flavour that bothers me, it's the texture. Little wrinkly and slimy raisins. Not to mention the sultanas, as well, slipping and sliding down your throat... EURRGH! NOPE! I can't even write anymore about them. It just makes me want to vom all over the paper. How am I going to do this??? PLEASE SEND HELP!!

Wrinkly SLIMY Raisin

'SPEW-DICULOUS' - ridiculously disgusting enough to make you want to be sick!

Slithering Sultana

Luckily, my mind was then distracted by the chocolate crispycakes, the gingerbread and the sugar cookies we made after the mince pies. Mmmmm!...The smell of cinnamon, vanilla and chocolate was AMAZING... Mince pie dread TOTALLY ANIHALATED! (FYI... That's a super-cool word that means destroyed on an EPIC scale).

Mum put some into a special box for when Elz comes over tomorrow along with a MINCE PIE each ... "WHAAAAT?!" I hear you say, I KNOW RIGHT? She said that I might change my mind and 'fancy' one ... ERRR NO MUM! I don't think so! I don't understand the way grown-ups think, do you? If you do let me know. I will be very grateful of the info.

EVIL MINCE PIE

PREP TIME

Elz came over yesterday morning with what looked like the contents of his entire bedroom. In his bag, along with the board games we usually play, he had packed some books all about elves and the legends of them. He thought we could read them to see if we could get some idea of what Crackers the elf would look like and where he may live.

Sadly, it didn't really give us any more information than the usual Christmas books do.

I told Elz I felt a bit worried that we hadn't told any of our mums about the notes. Let's face it, we don't actually know who this Crackers is, so he suggested that I tell my mum. So, I told her! I even showed her the notes from Crackers... but I really don't think she believed me AT ALL. She didn't tell me off or tell me that it wasn't true she just had that raised eyebrow look she gets when she doubts something and said, "That's lovely Charlie". I think she may have thought it was just a game we were playing. Even though I wasn't sure if she believed me, I felt better for doing the right, and the safest, thing by letting a grown-up know. So, with all that done we just had to wait.

It is now almost 11.45am on Christmas Eve. I am so nervous, I feel I may actually throw up. Not sure whether that's the dread of the mince pie or the not knowing of what is going to happen. I think Tommy can tell because he won't leave my side. Elz looks just as nervous. Just a few minutes more...

24 DEC

THIS IS WHAT HAPPENED

At midday, we opened the wardrobe door and, as promised, there sat two mince pies. But not just any mince pies... TWO MARVELLOUSLY MAGICAL MINCE PIES.

I passed one to Elz and held the other. I prepared myself to take that dreaded bite. Tommy looked up at me as *if* to say "Go on" so I took a huge bite. As me and Elz chewed the magical pie and I was waiting for that slimy sensation to start, I realized that it was NOTHING like the usual ones... NOT ONE WRINKLY RAISIN or a SLIMY SULTANA!! The *flavour* EXPLODED in my mouth. First it was gingerbread, then cinnamon; chocolate, then mint; eton mess, then marshmallow; Caramel and finally the UNMISTAKABLE SCRUMPLETASTIC *flavour* of my ONE and ONLY favourite chocolate... MARSHYMELTZ. That was NOTHING like a Mince Pie BUT the BEST MINCE PIE EVER!!!

In my utter delight at all the flavours, I failed to notice Tommy eating the crumbs that had fallen onto the floor. By the time I had realized what he was doing it was too late! As I reached down to stop him, there was a POPPING noise and he TOTALLY VANISHED. Panic filled me and I turned to ask Elz what we should do but then there was another POP and he was nowhere to be seen. I swallowed hard on the last piece of pie in my mouth, and it was then my whole room disappeared!

POP! POP!

Everything around me started spinning. It was all just a mix of colours like one of those kaleidoscope thingies you can get ... Psst! They're quite old so you may have to visit a museum to actually see one but my mum has one so that's how I know... I closed my eyes and waited for it to stop and that's when I felt a THUD followed by the sound of two more. When I opened my eyes, my bottom was sat in deep, thick, white snow. The snow started turning to slush as it was melting with the warmth of my bottom and my trousers got soggier with each second! Next to me, was Tommy, buried head first in the cold stuff. His legs were flailing in the air as he struggled to sit the right way up. Elz was sitting up waving and smiling. I was so relieved to see them again!

The longer we sat, the colder it seemed to get. We weren't prepared for the weather at all. Me and Elz were just wearing our tshirts and trousers and despite Tommy's thick fur, he sat there shivering with us too. As my bottom went from wet to TOTALLY NUMB like two frozen burgers from the supermarket, we decided that we should at least stand up. I picked Tommy up and brushed the snow from his face.

None of us were prepared for what followed next. I thought the Christmas Fayre was magical but this? THIS was SO much more magical-er! Ok that's probably not a real word but let's just put it in the Charlie Bottle dictionary of cool words for now, shall we?

MAGICAL-ER	Something that is a little more magical than the other magical thing.

Charlie Bottle Dictionary of Cool Words

I put Tommy on the ground. WOW... That cat is SUPER HEAVY. If I had carried him for any longer, my arms would have stretched like spaghetti.

Spaghetti Arms

Me, Elz and Tommy just stared at what was there in front of us. It was AMAZING! There were Christmas trees with bright colourful lights. The most magical ones I have ever seen!...

Lollipops were growing out of the ground like flowers.

There were other trees too. These ones were made of soft pink candyfloss and, on every candyfloss tree, branches stuck out to the side. On each and every branch sat a row of the tiniest houses EVER.

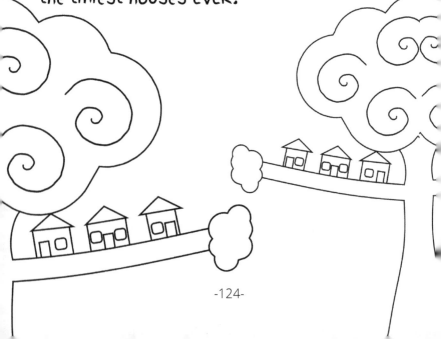

As we stood there, mouths wide open, gawping at the sight of such YUMMY candyfloss and wondering whether we should pick any from the trees, a strong wind seemed to push us forward along the path. Tommy hissed in disgust as his bottom lifted up from the floor pulling him away from the lollipop he had been, happily, licking. I pulled him towards me and grabbed on to Elz so we didn't get separated, but the wind seemed to want us to stay together. It tucked in around us and kept us close. I couldn't feel my feet touching the floor but we steadily moved along the path getting closer and closer to A GIGANTERIFFIC house!

This house had a HUMUNGOUS wooden door that greeted us at the end of the path. I mean it was HUGE!!!! I tried to lift the large letterbox flap like a door knocker to let someone know we were there but, there was NO way that I could because it was only my fingertips could touch it. It would have been far too heavy anyway. It turned out that I didn't even need to though, because, without warning, the MAHOUSIVE door flew wide open. I prepared myself for it to hit me as there was no way that we weren't going to be flung back into the snow by such a large door. But somehow (please don't ask me how as I have not got a clue) it didn't even touch us. It was as *if the* door went through us like ghosts. TOTALLY SPOOKY!

Tommy was so frightened, he puffed out into a giant furball and let off the loudest bottom-pop I have EVER heard. That made me do just one thing... Quickly point at him so that everyone knew it wasn't me!

I was very glad I cleared that matter up because, there in front of us stood Santa.

On closer inspection and after some "What are you doing Charlie?" looks from Elz, I realized that this Santa was THE REAL DEAL... 100% AUTHENTIC... THE BIG CHEESE! His beard was like a cloud of the FLUFFIEST marshmallows. His belly was all WIBBLY like jelly and his eyes disappeared behind his rosy cheeks when he smiled... His face cheeks not his bum cheeks... Rude (but totally funny!) haha!

Now where was I? Oh yeah that was it ...

I tried to say hello to him and even though I'm not sure that it even sounded anything like 'hello', Santa seemed to understand. I wasn't the only one that struggled to find the right words or even get them out of my mouth because Elz let out a high pitched SQUEAL which I can only assume would be translated into 'Hello Santa'. With Tommy's windy bottom, the new language that I had created which very few understood, as well as the sounds that were coming from Elz I don't think it was the best first impression we could have given The Big Man in red.

SANTA'S HOME

The warmth of Santa's home felt so good as we were FREEZING from being in the cold for so long. As we warmed up, my bottom no longer felt like frozen meatballs and my clothes started to dry. The hallway sparkled as the baubles, which hung around the hall, spun from the air that had followed us in through the door. There was a smell of fresh pine from the trees and it filled every inch. Well, I think it was pine because it smelled just like the toilet cleaner my mum uses. You know that green stuff? The one that has the advert where some crazy lady starts sniffing the air in a toilet and says something like "mmm pine fresh!"? I know, weird but true! Ok, where was I? Oh yes...

Tommy padded forward and wrapped his tail around the legs of Mrs Claus as she stood there with two large piles of warm winter clothes and one other smaller pile. Tommy was purring so loudly, it made her giggle and she handed over the two larger piles of warm, dry clothes to me and Elz. She took the smaller one which was a warm blanket and wrapped it around Tommy. Just when I was about to ask where we could change our clothes, Santa clicked his fingers and, suddenly, me and Elz were fully dressed in our new designer North Pole, TOTALLY TRENDY, winter clothes! Those clothes were so soft and cosy AND we got to take them home with us... RESULT!

We hadn't eaten for at least half an hour which meant that we were STARVING...OBVS! The food that had been put on a long table in front of us only confirmed how hungry we were when mine and Elz's tummies growled together, with perfect timing, at the sight of it. The table was HUMUNGOUS and filled with SCRUMMY looking treats. There were iced donuts, Gingerbread reindeers, Candy canes, chocolate muffins and there in all their heavenly glory sat a plate full of Santa's special Mince Pies!

With my eyes firmly fixed on the mince pies, we sat at the table where we were allowed to eat whatever we liked. OH YESSS!

But before I dived into those Mince Pies, I had to make sure that they were the same as the ones we ate earlier. You know, the ones with Gingerbread, Eton mess and MarshyMelts? Well... wait for it ...Santa told us that they were so SPECIAL that every bite was different! He said each one would taste like whatever foods we loved the most BUT these ones wouldn't make us travel anywhere else as they were missing that special ingredient. Reassured, by the big man, of guaranteed Mince Pie DELICIOUSNESS, me and Elz grabbed one each while Tommy plunged into a bowl of whipped cream especially for him.

OMG! the flavour was OUT OF THIS WORLD. This one started as MarshyMelts... I mean, come on, you must know by now that MarshyMelts will always be number one on my favourites list.

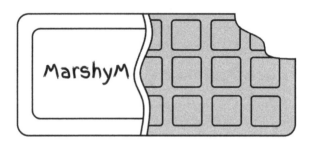

The second bite oozed with caramel and vanilla ice cream.

It was as cold as *ice cream* should be, just as though I had got a tub of the very stuff from the freezer. Pieces of curled white chocolate crunched in between my teeth as the sweetness exploded like fireworks on my tongue.

The third bite was strawberry jelly, custard and thick whipping cream just as a trifle should be. The jelly had just the right amount of wibble to its wobble reminding me of Mum's perfect trifle.

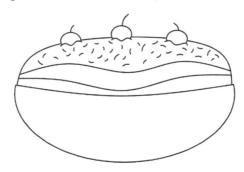

As mum's trifle filled my thoughts, as well as my tummy, I felt a wave of panic and the food, somehow, seemed harder to swallow! Mum had no idea where we were and neither did Elz's Mum. As I looked at Elz, I could see he felt the same too. Without a word Santa smiled at us and told us not to worry because he had paused time while we were with him and

Mrs Claus. Santa has some serious mind reading powers! But, TBH, I was really glad of them because now I knew that it meant when we returned it would be like we never left at all! The power of Magic is BAFFLING but AWESOME and, better still, it meant we could stay as long as we like without my mum worrying. Even Elz looked excited about us staying longer. He has truly conquered his fear of sleepovers... As his best friend I am SUPER PROUD of him!

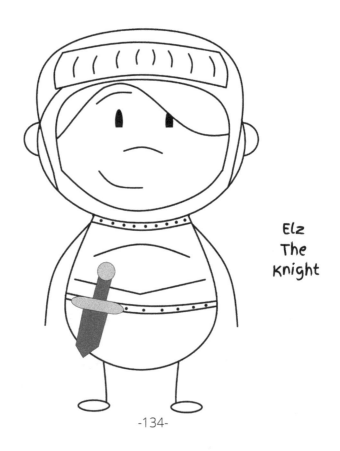

Elz
The
Knight

We completely lost track of the time. Feeling EXTREMELY stuffed from all the amazing food we had eaten, we moved from the table to the largest and SQUISHIEST sofas in the WHOLE WIDE WORLD.

SUPER SQUISHY SOFA
10/10 BOUNCE-ABILITY

The big man's living room was double the size of my house and we each had a sofa to ourselves! There was a tree decorated in lights, baubles and tinsel standing tall in the corner of the room. It wasn't anything like the tallest tree you have ever seen...

Imagine a tall tree... NOW triple that... NO... QUADRUPLE it. That's how big it was! Even a giant would say it was tall. At the top sat a really beautiful angel with snow white wings. I wish I could have shown mum, she would have loved her. It was fair to say this tree left me and Elz...

SPEECHLESS!

Our thoughts were broken when there was a knock at the door. As the door opened, we noticed it was getting dark. The Christmas lights seemed much brighter which made my tummy do that excited, twisty thing again. I couldn't see anyone standing at the door but I did hear a small voice say 'hello'. Santa invited them in and that was when we met Crackers for the first time. TBH, with all the magical stuff we had seen, I had COMPLETELY forgotten that we hadn't met Crackers the elf yet. I felt quite bad for forgetting him, so I said hello and waved as soon as I had the chance.

Crackers is about the size of my hand. He was dressed in a little green suit and a pointy hat, with a bright orange beard, and wore the shiniest black boots on rather big feet for such a small person.

As Crackers raised his small hand he froze like a statue. It was then I noticed that Tommy was purring loudly and getting closer to the little elf. Seeing that Crackers looked scared, I tried to pick Tommy up and move him away, but I was too late...Tommy licked the elf's face from the bottom of his beard, up past his ear and over the top of his hat. GROSS! Poor Crackers just stood there dripping in cat dribble. I CRINGED, not knowing what to say. I wanted to say something to make it better, but it was TOTALLY AWKWARD. It went so quiet. I held my breath waiting for someone to say something... anything at all... Finally, Santa let out a laugh as loud as thunder, which then made Crackers laugh and we all joined in. Well, all of us except Tommy who appeared to be TOTALLY in love with the elf.

To escape further washes in cat saliva, Crackers jumped up onto the table in the middle of the room where he placed his bottom in amongst a bowl filled with marshmallows... FYI, I did not eat any of said marshmallows thank you very much. EWW!

As we all sat snugly in our seats, Santa started coughing. At first, I thought he'd eaten one of those dodgy marshmallows but then I realized he was doing that throat noise that grown-ups make when they want to say something. What a relief, I had no idea how I was supposed to do that Heimlich thingy on the big guy!

BTW I'm not being mean, but Santa is SO tall...let's just say I didn't stand behind him just in case.

The room went silent waiting for Santa to speak. It was then he explained to us why he had been looking for a 'kind and thoughtful' child. He told us that this year he had noticed something unusual on his GOOD-O-METER. He said that the light had been blinking on and off like crazy which meant only one thing... that there was a child (or in this case, two) who went above and beyond what was needed to be on the

GOOD list. He had sent Crackers to investigate because he has SUPER AWESOME Detective skills, like mine.

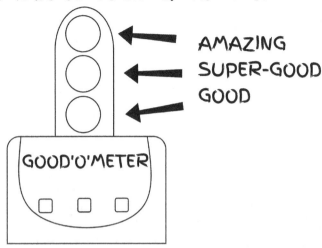

AMAZING
SUPER-GOOD
GOOD

GOOD'O'METER

That's when he found me and Elz. I couldn't believe that we had made the Good-o-meter go into overdrive. This reward was AMAZE-BALLS, GROOVYRIFFIC, AWESOMETASTIC AND TOTALLY OUT OF THIS WORLD! On Christmas eve morning, we had NO idea, that by the afternoon, we would be standing in the same room as THE BIG CHIEF OF THE FLYING REINDEER!

Santa explained that because me and Elz look after each other and we take the time to look after those that need a friend, our friend Ship is special. When I tried to explain to him that we didn't have a ship, he just smiled and said that 'friend ship' was one word (friendship) and that it was another word to explain being friends.

I thought this was really cool but, once again losing track of thought, I still couldn't get the image of us as swashbuckling pirates out of my head. OOH ARRRGGGH, ME MATEYS!

WE BE HUNTING TREASURE!

REINDEER FUN-DER

I woke up the next morning in the most softest bed ever. I still couldn't quite believe that it was all real but as I looked at the room that me and Elz had slept in, there was NO WAY that I had made it up. There was also one other thing that made me believe that it was real... and that's the fact I KNOW my mum doesn't snore. It is very clear now that Santa does! It was so loud, not only could I hear it in our room but, my dream turned from being all about Christmas and toys to one that involved being chased by Jurassic Pigs!

Jurassic
Pig -
The
Sabre Tooth
Snorer

Thank goodness it was a dream because those pigs were SUPER scary!

I made a note to myself to put something over my ears for the rest of the nights that we were staying. Elz does it and he seemed to sleep through the choir of killer pigs so I was sure it would help me too. I wasn't wrong either.

Elz woke up a little later than me. I think it was the smell of warm sugar waffles with chocolate and strawberries that woke him. It seemed to fill the whole house ... EVERY SINGLE TINY MILLIMETRE of it. We followed the sweet scented air down the stairs and found sugary waffles, DRIZZLED (FYI, another AWESOME word) with chocolate sauce, stacked high on the table in the kitchen. They looked like mini skyscrapers and the table was a city made of all things SCRUMPTIOUS.

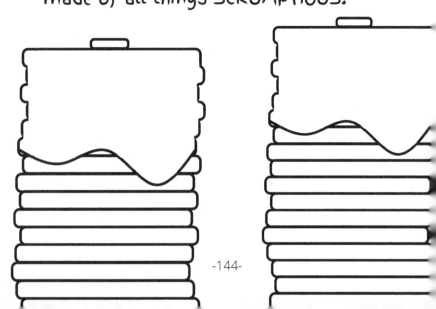

The chocolate flowed in one of those posh fountain thingies that my uncles had at their wedding, and right next to it sat a bowl piled high with the plumpest, reddest and most juiciest looking strawberries I've ever seen! TOTAL HEAVEN!

We couldn't *fill* our plates fast enough with all the goodies! Mrs Claus poured warm milk and honey into two large Christmas mugs for us and some into a giant silver mug for Santa. A large newspaper that read 'North Pole News' covered his face but when he saw us, he folded it and placed it on the table next to him. His eyes twinkled just like they do in the pictures, on those really fancy christmas cards. They got wider as he looked at all the food , then filled his plate just like we had. The table fell silent as we feasted on the WAFFLE-TASTIC food. After we had licked every single crumb and chocolate smudge off of our plates, we put on our warm, new coats and headed out into the snow. When I stepped out and looked around I was surprised to see that the trees, that were there when we had arrived, had moved. It was as *if the* trees had legs and just walked away. Thinking it was because I was a little confused after all the events so far, I didn't mention it to anyone.

Tommy softly padded across my shoulders where he tucked himself, as deep as he could, into my hood to keep warm. He finally FLOMPED into what I can only guess was a sleeping position there. I tried to remain standing as his ROYAL FLUFFBALL who, BTW had also just eaten

adding more OOMPH to his snuggle impact, relaxed and added all his weight to my hood. I bent forward to try and balance out the extra weight by sticking my bottom up in the air as we trudged through the snow to the reindeer ranch.

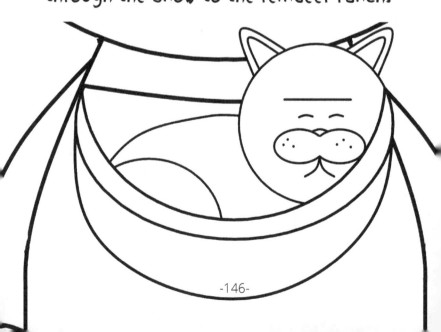

When we finally arrived at the Reindeer ranch, my mouth hung open at the sight in front of us. When The Big Guy said 'ranch' I don't know why, but I just imagined your average sized animal barn, but it really did live up to the name! This ranch, the one the reindeer live in, was like an ULTIMATE, SUPER-DELUXE MANSION. It was bigger than Santa's house! But when we stepped inside it was obvious why. When people tell you that Santa has eight reindeer, don't believe them. He has twenty-four! I'll start with the names you may already know but here the first twelve names:

DASHER   BLITZEN

DANCER   DONNA

PRANCER

VIXEN   CUPID

COMET

STORM   VOLT

WAVE   SLAY

Now you are probably wondering what the other twelve are, and I will tell you, I promise, but I just want to say I really feel like Santa may have got a bit lost when he chose the other twelve names as they are as follows:

BOB GORDON
JEFFREY ROB
BRIAN NIGEL KEVIN
(Not the Nose Picker one)

MAVIS HAROLD JIM

MARMADUKE MABLE

See what I mean? Don't get me wrong they're not bad names but 'Bob the flying reindeer' doesn't quite have the same ring to it and sound as awesome as 'Storm the flying reindeer', does it?

We spent the whole day in and around the reindeer barn getting to know all the reindeer.

1. Dasher - Quick like his name but VERY clumsy.

2. Dancer - pretty much away with the fairies (not real ones just a phrase).

3. Prancer - Dancer's twin in looks and personality.

4. Vixen - Sarcastic but funny.

5. Comet - REALLY BRAINY! I wish I could take him to school with me.

6. Cupid - Completely chilled out.

7. Donna - Loves to play games especially that one where you have to put your foot on one colour circle and then another part of your body on another circle until you get so tangled up, you end up wobbling and falling over.

8. Blitzen - TOTALLY obsessed with keeping things clean and tidy - Spent the whole time cleaning up after everyone making sure that nothing looked messy.

9. Storm - The ULTRA COOL one - He even wore shades for added coolness.

STORM

10. Wave - Totally chilled snowboarder and his favourite word was 'dude'!

11. Volt - I'm not sure how I can put this other than... He's BARMY-BAUBLES... A TOTAL FESTIVE-FRUITCAKE...But so funny and still one of my favourites.

12. Slay - He is the one that follows Storm around and pretty much copies everything he does. He even wears the same shades.

13. Bob - Loves reading and listening to that fancy 'classical' music that grown-ups love.

14. Jeffrey - Now, Jeffrey is a little bit serious and with that trait he adds a little bit of grump whereas ...

15. Gordon - is also serious but worries LOADS which makes him very nervous.

16. Brian - is like what I imagine a good dad would be like if you turned him into a reindeer. A total all round good guy and ready to help in as soon as asked.

17. Rob - A huge sports fan. He said his favourite sport is TinselTrotters which is their version of football or hoofball. Really hard to watch with all the skinny reindeer legs scrambling everywhere. Sometimes it's hard to spot the ball amongst all the hoofs.

18. Kevin - KEVIN THE KARATE REINDEER - A tinsel belt in karate and Santa's protector.

19. Nigel - Thankfully not like Nigel in my class. Although I'm not quite sure how a reindeer would actually be able to pick his nose with hoofs unless he had SUPER HUGE NOSTRILS. BUT here is how I think he might look if he did... (sorry Nigel!).

20. Harold - has his own reindeer kitchen where he creates new recipes. He says he would like to be a famous chef one day like you see on the TV. I told him he would have to practice shouting at people because that's what they do quite a lot on the programme mum watches. I also told him that he needs to practice the 'bleep' noise that they keep making whilst shouting. He got quite good at it by the time we left.

21. Jim - The Buff Reindeer - constantly working out in his homemade gym. When I saw the sign above where he was lifting his weights, I did tell him that the gym is not spelled like 'Jim' but he insisted that he was right. Well, it wasn't hurting anyone and he seemed to love it so I wasn't going to go all 'Mrs MoodyPants' on him.

22. Mavis - The 'Singer' of the group. It wasn't until we met Mavis did we realise why exactly we were told to wear discrete earplugs. On careful, but subtle, inspection I notice that the only ones in there without them was Mavis and ...

23. Mable - who had lost her hearing one

year when they *flew* over fireworks display at the Grand Canyon. Apparently a FizzyFrantic FireFlipping FizzWizzle exploded near her ear and she hasn't been able to hear since then. She said that was ok because all the other reindeer have been so kind and they have learned to talk in sign language. I think I might try and learn to do sign language too so, *if I ever* meet someone who can't hear, I will be able to make them *feel* more included when everyone is talking. Besides it's a SERIOUSLY COOL language to learn too.

24. Marmaduke - The Gassy Reindeer - Apparently this causes quite a bit of chaos on Christmas eve as there is a bit of a SHOWDOWN as to where he should be among the other reindeer at the front of the sleigh. Santa said he insists that he should be at the very front and the reindeer beg for him to be at the back. TBH, I can completely understand both sides of this argument.

Please just know I was not fully aware of Marmaduke's parping posterior when Santa said that the reindeers had offered to take us *flying...*

So Elz chose Storm and, yes you guessed it, I chose Marmaduke! I was so excited at the thought of being taken to the skies by the most magical flying beings in the entire galaxy that Tommy and I climbed onto Marmaduke's back without any suspicion and held on to the special reins he was wearing. As we sat there noticing how sparkly his reindeer fur was, we heard an almighty EXPLOSION from his rear and we shot off into the sky. Tommy pierced my coat with his claws as he tried desperately to hold on and somehow, I managed to pull him in close to me and keep him safe.

No matter how much I held on to the reins or how safe I was keeping Tommy with him tucked away in my coat, nothing and I mean NOTHING...ZILCH...NIL...ABSOLUTELY NADA could stop the stench that followed. I watched the grey colour of Tommy's fur drain into more of a greenish grey as his eyes started to water. At the same time my gag reflex was triggered. I knew it hadn't been long since we had eaten so, making sure Tommy was safe, I placed my scarf over my nose and mouth to stop me from becoming the first ever waffle fountain.

As the heaving stopped, and my nose was protected from the frequent gas leaks from Marmaduke's bottom, he flew us on a tour of the North Pole. A thick blanket of snow covered most of the ground below but sparkles from the magic that hung on almost everything made it far more magical than you can ever imagine. Tommy settled and I wasn't sure whether he had fallen asleep under my coat, or he had passed out from Reindeer stench.

I'm not sure how long we were up there in the skies, but by the time Marmaduke crash landed into the nearest bush, the sun was starting to go down. Elz said he had completely forgotten about lunch as he was having so much fun. But seeing as I never forget about food, I can only assume that Marmaduke's butt had killed several of my brain cells causing temporary memory loss. With my memory, once again, working with a full set of cells I was ready for more food. Luckily, Mrs Claus thinks just like me because she had set out a picnic, for us all, in the ranch.

Giant Cake

Strawberries

Apples

Sandwiches

We spent the rest of the evening playing party games with the reindeer but, when it started to get much colder as night fell, we made our way back to Santa, Mrs Claus and the warmth of their home.

When we approached the house, I noticed that the trees were back where we had first seen them. This made me 100% sure that they really did move. When I asked the Big Guy he said, "That's why we call it The Wandering Forest" and laughed. He also said, "Some elves have to sleep here some nights because their houses wander with the trees and they just can't find them!" and chuckled some more. That must be so confusing. Imagine living somewhere and going home only to see that its not there anymore because it's got up and walked off. What if my house decided to have a stroll and put itself next to Beatrice's house????... Beatrice would become my neighbour... What if it put itself next to Mrs Moody's house??... The HORROR!!!!

GAMER-TIME

The next morning, we were woken by the sound of sleigh bells outside the window. At first, I thought we were going to go on a SERIOUSLY FESTIVE MAGICAL ride in the sleigh but what greeted us outside was far from it. It wasn't in a disappointing way though but more of a jingly bells kind of way. Apparently, according to Crackers, it's traditional for elves to wear bells on their clothes when spending the day with guests at the North Pole. A slightly strange tradition but I suppose some of the stuff humans do must seem strange to them too. We are all different so there's no way I am going to judge.

Crackers doesn't seem that big on conversation, just the odd little squeak or grunt. I think he might have been a little nervous around us but then again, I think he might have just been nervous around Tommy. I know Tommy loves him, but he is much, MUCH bigger than Crackers, it would be like having a giant lion following you and I would definitely be nervous if that happened to me!

Crackers took us to the Toy workshop. The size of it didn't surprise me at all. I always assumed it had to be bigger than Santa's home and the reindeer ranch so it only seemed right that it was almost four times the size of where the reindeer live.

Inside of the ranch was another story... The shelves were stacked all the way to the ceiling. They covered every inch of the walls. As well as those, there were huge toy bins filled with plush, cuddly, soft toys. I wondered if one of those would be for Melly. They looked so squishy and I knew she would love one. There were other rooms that lead off the main area and one of those I knew I had to explore ... THE GAMING ROOM... AWESOME!!!!

GAMING IN PROGRESS

KEEP OUT

As we walked around the main area, and I was trying to distract my thoughts from the gaming room, I noticed that the elves had a SUPER, but somewhat strange, talent. They were bouncing for every movement like it was the only way to get around. I don't mean tiny jumps like 'wee-boing' I am talking PRO ATHLETE SUPER DOOPER BOUNCYRIFFIC BOINGY STYLE!

I watched as they bounced to and from where they needed to be and then it all made sense. It was totally obvs that bouncing was the only way they could reach so high and as soon as the toys were made, they had to be stacked on those shelves or put into the baskets that were meant for them. It was then I decided that it was very AWESOME skill especially if you are as small as an elf.

We caught sight of the one thing me and Elz wanted so badly being carried, one by one, to the room I spotted earlier. So that took my eyes back to the GAMING ROOM. We watched each zSPHERES disappear into that room for testing and as the door opened, we could hear the sounds of the EPIC games being played. Even though I knew that I hadn't asked Santa for one, and I really just wanted a phone for my mum, I still wanted to try it out even if for only a little while.

By now, to Tommy's frustration, Crackers was riding on his back , buried deep in his fur. It was pretty genius really because not only did he ride in style, but

Tommy couldn't turn around and reach him to lick him again. I was just a bit concerned that Tommy would suddenly FLOMP down on the floor like he does and poor Crackers would be crushed beneath him...

Crackers guided Tommy forward, edging toward the gaming room where he showed us in and gestured for us to sit with the other elves and play... OMG ... What a GAME-MAZING afternoon.

I'm not sure how long we were gaming for but, when we finally looked up from it, we saw Santa standing over us saying that it was dinner time and we had to go back to their home. We thanked Crackers and all the gaming elves and made our way back.

I have never heard Elz so chatty as he was after that. He told Santa all about how amazing he thinks the ZSpheres is and all the games that you can play on it too. Santa asked if I would like one for Christmas but that was when I said that I did but what I really wanted was a phone for my mum and I also mentioned the teddy bear for Melly. He told us that he would make a note of it but we would have to wait and see what he leaves under the tree on Christmas eve. Once again, when he said that, my tummy did that twisty turny feeling again with excitement but, this time, I noticed another feeling with it. It was something I didn't like. It made me feel sad. It was then I realized that I was missing my mum and sister. So that night I asked Elz if he was missing home as much as I was. I was so relieved when he said yes because it meant that we were

both ready to leave. We both agreed that,
tomorrow, we would ask Santa if we could
return home.

THE LAST DAY

We woke up early the next morning ready to ask Santa *if we could* go home that day. TBH, I was really dreading it because I thought that by asking, I may upset him and everyone there. They had been so kind to us so, it was the last thing we wanted to do. Much to my relief, Santa totally understood. He also said that the magic to pause time couldn't have lasted much longer anyway and it was probably for the best.

Before we left the North Pole for good, with Tommy snuggled up by the warmth of the log fire, Santa and Mrs Claus took us to the top of Blizzard Hills. Blizzard hills was a lot calmer than you think it would be with a name like that. In fact, there wasn't a blizzard in sight. What we did find though were lots and lots of Snowmen and twenty-four reindeer waiting for us to join them.

Just to the side of the hills, propped up in a pile against the trees, were wooden sleds ready and waiting for all of us. OMG...AWESOME. Sledding in the most Christmassy place in the world!

To see snowmen walking about, laughing and talking was OUT OF THIS WORLD. It made me wonder whether the ones that we build, in our world, do the same thing in secret? Can you imagine that? In the middle of the night when you are fast asleep that your snowman goes wandering around all the roads and you just have NO IDEA? Not even a teeny tiny clue? AWESOME!! Quick note to self... never build a snowman of Beatrice, Mrs Moody or The Phantom Nosepicker because one each of those is quite enough thank you very much!

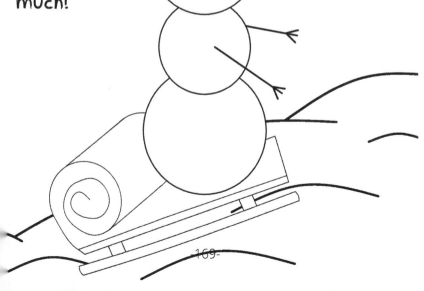

We met all of the snowmen that day at the top of the hill. There was:

Seth:

Sydney:

Eric:

Wallace:

Ernie:

Ethel:

Phyllis:

Henry:

Albert:

Rosie:

Charles:

Percy:

Harold:

And

Stanley:

All the snowmen lined up at the top of the hill with the reindeer gathered at the side as our audience. I spotted Marmaduke waving a flag with my name on it and Storm with another flag with 'Elz' painted on it. We weren't just going to be sledding, we were going to have a race!

We each grabbed a sled and positioned ourselves at the very top of Blizzard hill. I noticed Santa stretching like athletes do. He was even wearing a sweat band on his head and one on each of his wrists. I could see that the Big guy meant business.

Mrs Claus was taking it seriously too. She was dressed in those tight trousers mum calls Yoga Pants, a thick winter coat, ski goggles and sweat bands on her head and wrists. When I looked at the snowmen standing around us, I realized that the only competition that there seemed to be was between Santa and Mrs Claus.

When they had finished warming up, for what clearly was a competition for them, they sat down on their sleds and edged to the very peak of the hill with the rest of us. Elz looked nervous so I promised him he would be ok. We both took the ropes of our sleds and waited for the whistle to start.

As the whistle blew, I paddled with my feet in the snow to push me forward on the sled. Within seconds the sled took control, and I tucked my feet up out of the way. As I shot down the hill like a rocket, I quickly looked beside me and noticed Elz was right there with a huge smile across his face.

NORTH POLE SLED CO.   NORTH POLE SLED CO.

On the other side, Santa shot past like lightning. He was just a huge flash of red and white. Following closely behind him was Mrs Claus who was now standing on the sled with her bottom sticking out and two of those stick thingies skiers use pushing her forward. I think she may actually be the world's biggest cheat doing it like that! Lolz

On the other side the snowmen whizzed down the hill. Some were behind us and some in front. Seth the snowman fell off his sled and continued down the hill just by rolling. By the time he reached the

bottom of the hill he was no longer a snowman. He was now a HUMUNGOUS snowball.

When the first race ended, we were all buzzing with excitement. There were a few broken twigs here and there, from the snowmen, but thankfully the reindeer had already thought of that because next to them was a box marked 'Spare arms'.

Spare Arms

Seth rolled himself to the side next to the box and started shaking off the excess snow so now he was back to his old snowself.

Santa was lying in the snow in fits of laughter. Me and Elz were a bit confused and had no idea what he was laughing at. When we asked him, he managed to point up at a tree inbetween gasps of belly laughter. There in the tree, upside down, hanging from her feet was Mrs Claus. Apparently, she had a hit a bump on the snow when she was standing on the sled and it threw her up into the tree. LOLZ!

The reindeer started scooping up the snow and placing it just underneath where she was hanging until eventually there was a small hill beneath her. Mrs Claus slowly released her foot from the branch and dropped safely down onto the mound of snow where she let out a loud laugh, popped her goggles and sweatband back on, and called out "That was fun! Let's do it again!" So off she trudged back up the hill.

The morning carried on that way, although Mrs Claus was careful not to land in the tree again. It was TOTALLY FUN and by the end of it, as much as we still wanted to go home, there was part of me that wanted to stay just so that we could go sledding again.

We put all the sleds away and said goodbye to the snowmen and the reindeer. We thanked them for spending time with us and making us feel so welcome. They told us that they would miss us and I know that I am missing them too as I write this. We then popped into the toy workshop to say goodbye to the elves and of course the AMAZINGLY COOL Zsphere 5 gaming room... Maybe next year I will ask Santa for one.

I think Crackers had grown to love Tommy as much as Tommy loved him because he returned to Santa's house with us to say his final goodbyes.

When we arrived back at Santa's home, Tommy was still curled up and purring loudly by the fireplace. It was warm and cozy in there so I couldn't blame him at all. Woken by the noise we were making, he  slowly stretched out like cats do from the tips of his front claws all the way to the top of his tail as he displayed his bottom to all... FYI, Cat's should wear underpants... just saying. On his final stretch he stood up and padded towards me, gently picked crackers up with his teeth and carefully flung him up onto his back where Crackers laid flat in his fur. The elf stretched out his arms wide, wrapped them as far as they would go around Tommy and stayed there for a while just to show Tommy how much he was going to miss him by giving him a huge hug. As he wiped away a tear, Crackers slid down the side of Tommy, back onto the floor. I scooped Tommy up and placed him inside my coat while Mrs Claus fetched us a Mince Pie each.

When she returned she was carrying two normal size mince pies and a smaller one the size of a cat treat.

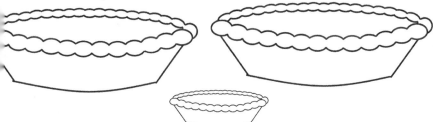

Tommy quickly gobbled the treat size mince pie and just like that 'POP' he was gone.

Before I bit into mine, I remembered to sat
thank you to Santa and Mrs Claus for
letting us stay with them and for all the
fun that we'd had. Elz did the same, then
together we both bit into our magical
mince pies.

As the caramel, chocolate and shortbread flavours of the mince pie passed over my tongue, the room and the people around me disappeared out of sight. Colours broke into patterns like shards of glass. I knew I was on my way home.

Then, with a pop, I was back in my bedroom standing in front of Elz and Tommy sitting at my feet. We were home.

I checked the clock, which has both the time and date on it, to see what it said. Sure enough, it was just like Santa had said because it was exactly the same time and date that we had left.

24 DEC

Everything inside me made me want to run down to see my mum and just give her a big SQUEEZY hug but I knew that no time had passed for Mum, and it would just make her suspicious, so I just casually walked down into the kitchen to get a drink for me and Elz. I was so happy to see her and Melly sitting together at the kitchen table.

By this time Elz was desperate to go and see his mum so, he wished Mum and Melly a happy christmas and we walked together back to his home.

We decided to keep all of this a secret just between us and never to be discussed with anyone else. Totally TOP SECRET! If we told the other kids in our class, they would just say that we were making it up. I don't want anybody putting any doubts into my head over what actually happened, and I knew that if the kids in our class kept saying that we made it up I would just start questioning myself and wondering whether I had imagined the whole thing! ... I really don't want to forget or disbelieve the magic that we have just been a part of and most of all, question the magical and amazing friends that we have made.

Later when I got home, I went back upstairs and put the coat and scarf from the North Pole away into my wardrobe. I tucked them at the back for safe keeping and tidied up my room. Tommy hadn't moved from my bed. It looked like our festive trip had absolutely exhausted him so I left him to rest some more. I was just excited to spend the rest of the day with Mum and Melly. I went downstairs and sat at the kitchen table with them. I was ready for all the Christmas Eve fun that lay ahead.

OH YES I DID!

The afternoon *flew* by as we cleared the house ready for the big day. We blew up balloons, like mum said we would, and placed three in every corner of the living room. We tied some to the banisters on the stairs and hung a *few* on ribbons from the ceiling. We hung them in most rooms except the kitchen and the bathroom. There is something about balloons that just make me *feel* so much more excited for tomorrow.

Mum *filled* bowls with sweets and covered them them with *foil* to stop them from getting ruined. Every Christmas, we have a little side table where these go and next to them are bottles of *fizzy* pop. I used to crouch behind the sofa and sneak a few out but I think Mum may have noticed as she moved the sofa and now I have nowhere to hide... TRADITION TOTALLY DESTROYED. How am I going to teach Melly now?

with the whole house now *fully* CHRISTMASFIED (another new word for my book). I thought we were going to spend the evening munching on goodies and watching the usual Christmas movies, but mum had other plans for us. She told me that she had a surprise, that I should get myself ready and to 'wear something smart but warm'. I put on my favourite Christmas jumper and a pair of jeans, grabbed my coat, my reindeer antlers and met Mum and Melly in the hallway. I had no idea where we were going and Mum was keeping the surprise very secret.

It was dark out and I was pleased I'd put my jumper on under my coat because somehow it seemed colder outside in the evening than it did during the day.

It didn't *feel* like we travelled very far in the car, but when Mum showed us where we had stopped, I knew we had gone further than I thought. We were standing in front of the town's theatre. I had never been there before today, but I definitely knew what it was.

Every year at Christmas they put on a pantomime, and I have always wanted to see one. I never thought it would happen though. They always put on a new play each year created by people locally, so I was really excited to see this year's one.

As we entered the foyer (BTW that's the posh word for the big room as you enter the building) I couldn't believe how big it was. I knew that it was big from the outside but being inside the theatre just made it seem HUMUNGOUS. The ceilings were so high up and you should have seen the stairs we had to climb to get to our seat in the theatre. Climbing those was like a P.E lesson at school when the teacher is in an extra bad mood. I mean I'm all for a surprise, but I never knew that I would have to sweat for it!

We finally made it to our seat but when we got there a person that worked there asked us if we could sit closer to the front. Obviously, we were very happy with that, but it would have been better if they had told us before we had climbed all those stairs. So back down the stairs we went to our new seats where we could see all the stage. It was a TOTALLY EPIC move for us.

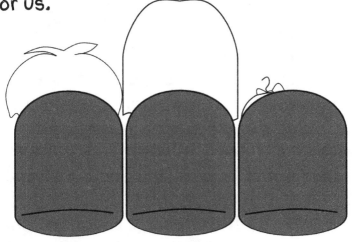

When the lights dimmed and we were hidden, Mum pulled out some treats she had smuggled in the theatre from the inside of her bag... ummmmm Naughty Mum... I know, BUT SERIOUSLY have you seen the prices of the snacks they sell in the foyer??? Mum can't afford those! It would have been hard for her just getting enough money for our tickets so this was the only way we could afford treats. We had popcorn, jelly sweets, crisps and custard filled donuts!! AWESOME!!! The smell of the donuts wafted up my nose and made my tummy growl so loudly the man in 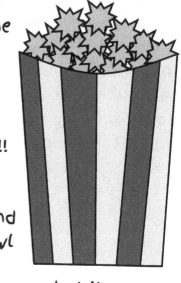 front of me turned to see what it was. Obviously, it was my duty to make sure that I didn't make such a noise again so I unwrapped the biggest SQUIDGIEST custard donut I could find and bit straight into it. It was DONUTTY-CUSTARDLY-AWESOME! By its silence I could tell that my tummy agreed too.

PLUMP AND SQUIDGY DONUT

Up on the stage, all the lights went on and the curtains opened to reveal the set. I had never seen one like that before. The sets at school always look like they got into a physical fight with all the parts half taped on and half hanging off! But this stage was something else. It was BRILLIANT!

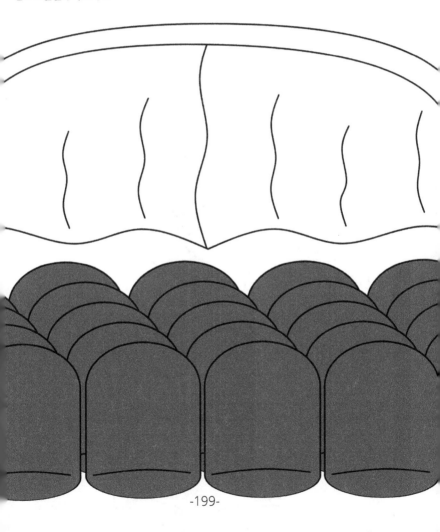

Music started playing and a lady walked out onto the stage. She was dressed in a big, puffy dress with thick, curly hair piled on top of her head and she wore the brightest make-up I have ever seen. Mum said she is known as a 'Pantomime Dame' or 'Panto Dame' for short. Whatever she's called, I thought she was BRILLIANT!

PANTO
DAME

She called out to all of us in the audience to ask if we had seen her pet dragon. She said she couldn't find him but he was secretly following her. As loud as we could, we shouted "He's behind you!". She did find him eventually but every time she turned around to look, he hid. When she realised that he had been behind her the whole time, she chased him off the stage for being naughty. It was so funny, and the dragon was really cool.

For most of the pantomime the audience were laughing but, like most stories, there was always going to be a mean character and this story's one was an evil wizard. He had a long pointy nose and he was wearing a green cloak and hat. He wanted to take the dragon away from the lady so he kept trying to steal him.

It wasn't a sad pantomime though because the dragon was too smart and AWESOME to be fooled by the wizard. I wonder if dragons are real. Imagine how EPIC it would be to know one and be friends with them! That would be MEGA EPIC!

The pantomime was BRILLIANT! I loved every moment of it, especially when they threw sweets out into the audience. BTW, this was another bonus of being closer to the stage because all the sweets landed near the front rows where we were. As the sweets fell, I grabbed a few. I got some soft ones for Melly, some for Mum and me but, I also noticed that there was a girl with a disability who wasn't able to get any of them, so I grabbed some for her too. She was really pleased when I gave the sweets to her and that made me happy.

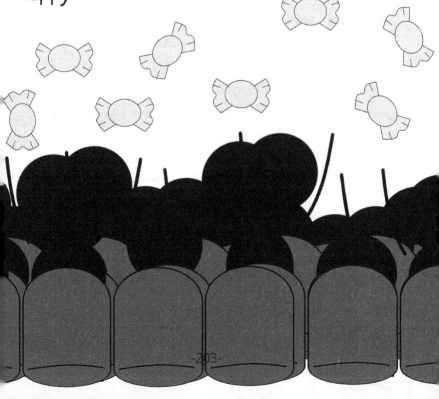

When the show ended everyone clapped, whistled and cheered. It wasn't because they were pleased it had ended, because that would just be rude. They did it because they had loved the show. It's kind of like a 'thank you'. My mum said it is "A show of appreciation". She said that people make a booing sound when they don't like a show. Wow! Can you imagine working so hard acting infront of an audience and then they boo at you? That would make me so sad. In fact, I think I would cry forever. Mum says that to treat people the right way you should imagine how the words you want to say and the things you want to do would affect you if someone did the same to you and then decide whether that it is kind or not. I have decided that booing someone is definitely NOT a nice thing to do.

When the curtains closed and the set on the stage could no longer be seen, we gathered up all that we'd bought with us and shuffled out of the theatre as everyone else was leaving too. What a SQUEEEEEEZE! When we finally found the main entrance door, I let out a huge sigh of relief. No-one was bumping into me anymore, and I could finally move about freely. It was so much colder and darker when we made our way back to the car. Luckily, mum had parked really close because it felt so eerie. I had visions of big monsters coming out of the bushes. I know there wasn't any there but my imagination would not be quiet and kept trying to tell me that there was. Just the tiniest sound made my heart beat super fast. I held onto Mum's hand tightly and kept close to her just in case!

Obviously as I am writing this, I'm at home which also means it is nearly the time for me to sleep. I am MEGA excited for Christmas and my brain won't be quiet about it... How am I going to get to sleep like this?? My brain is literally replaying all the events of the last few days as well as reminding me of all the worries I have. I'm even reliving the most annoying moments with Beatrice in my brain, telling her what I wanted to say to her rather than what I actually did. I really want to sleep though because Mum says Santa won't be able to deliver if I don't. So here goes, I am going to try to sleep... wish me luck.

Night guys!

CHRISTMAS DAY

I can't wait to tell you all about today. I am not entirely sure why, but I fell asleep SUPER QUICK last night! I can't even remember closing my eyes. Well, obviously, I did close my eyes but all I know is that one minute I was in bed worrying how I was going to sleep, and then the next it was Christmas morning. Don't ask me how I managed that because I have not got a clue, but it has to be a first for me. When I woke up, Mum was calling out "Merry Christmas!" to me and Melly. She gets just as excited about Christmas as I do. I jumped out of bed and quicky made my way downstairs to the living room where she and Melly were waiting for me. All the presents with their shiny, glittery paper sat under the tree. I asked Mum if I could sort the presents into piles... One pile for me, one for Melly and one for Mum. I was desperate to see whether there was something there for Mum that looked like it may be the phone I asked Santa for. Looking baffled by how eager I was, she chuckled and said yes so,

I dived straight in and began. There were a few presents but, at the back, sat three presents with identical paper, tags and golden bows. I instantly knew they were from Santa.

There was a squishy looking present for Melly...

a mobile phone sized one for Mum (EeeeeeKK!!!!!)...

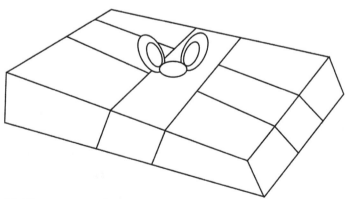

AND...

A large one for me............

I had no idea what it could be because it seemed like he had given Mum the phone I had asked for and I hadn't asked for anything else. Although I was REALLY excited, it did make me worry that maybe Mum hadn't got the phone. I quickly handed the present to her and waited for her to open it so I could find out. I was SO relieved when she unwrapped a BRAND NEW ULTIMATE SUPER TECHY mobile phone.

You should have seen her face. She was so surprised and happy. She said I should open mine next as Melly was already squishing and squeezing her new teddy bear. Well, I don't need to be told twice! I tore off the bow and then the paper, strip by strip. As each strip of missing paper revealed a little more of what was underneath, I held my breath. I couldn't believe what I was seeing. Bright blue metallic letters printed across the box of the one thing every kid, in my class, hoped for this christmas. I tried not to get my hopes up too high because my mum often puts gifts inside boxes just for packaging so maybe that's what Santa had done but when I actually opened the box there inside sat the MOST AWESOME, MOST AMAZING and MOST GAMERIFFIC gift EVER... the Zsphere 5!!!!!!!!!!!!!!!!!!

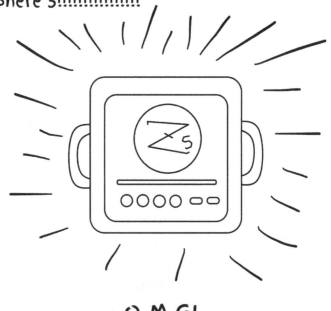

O.M.G!

In my rush to see what it was I hadn't read the tag properly but when I looked again I read...

"To Charlie, something just for you because you always think of others. We hope you like it. Love from Santa and all at the North Pole"

I looked over at Mum. I could see she was just as surprised as I was. As we unwrapped the rest, Mum took photos of us all with the camera on her new phone. Some of my other presents were:

1. A Giant *fluffy* hoodie. One of those ones that are so big they go down past your knees.

2. Soft *fluffy* reindeer slippers.

3. Crayons, pens, pencils and a sketch pad.

4. A new diary.

DIARY

5. A cuddly teddy bear

AND ....

8. Santa had left one more present for me. This time it wasn't from him. The tag said it was a special gift from Crackers...

A bundle of games for my Zsphere 5...

AWESOME!!!

Crackers had been really generous because he had left a special present for Tommy too. It didn't take Tommy long to get to what was inside. I think he knew exactly what it was because he had already ripped most of the paper off and was sitting in a pile of it. Melly found this super funny. She was giggling away, especially when he kicked it up in the air, pounced on it and then turned back to the treats that was inside the paper and try to eat them without taking them out of the pouch they were in. Crazy Fluffball! HAHA!

By the time all the gifts were open, there was wrapping and packaging all over the floor. I helped mum collect it all up and put it in the bin so we could get on with the day.

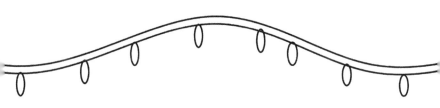

Nan and Grandad visit us every Christmas day and they have dinner with us too. It wouldn't be the same without them. I was already planning how I was going to hide my sprouts. My usual trick is to hide them in the potatoes...

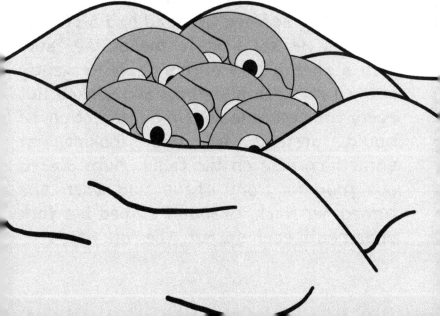

But after mum discovered my hiding place last year I don't think I will get away with that again. So now I had to either:

1. Be brave and eat the nasty things while trying not to spew all over my plate.

Or ...

2. Find somewhere else to hide them. A place where Mum will NEVER find them.

The thought of putting just one of those evil things in my mouth was TOO much and it was then I realized I had no choice but to come up with a better hiding place! But when it came to that dreaded moment, it seemed Grandad had a plan of his own. He sat next to me at the table with a cheeky grin on his face. He gently nudged me with his elbow and winked but every time mum looked in our direction, he would pretend he was looking at something else on the table. Mum placed our food in front of us and when she turned her back, Grandad swiped his fork underneath each sprout. The fork lifted the sprout up into the air. Each one swiftly flew from my plate like a mini football, that had just been kicked, and landed neatly on Grandad's mashed potato as it's intended goal. You should have seen the precision. If there was an award for the best played game with sprouts, my grandad would win a Gold Medal!

When Mum noticed that the sprouts had gone, she told me how pleased she was that I had eaten them. I didn't agree because it would feel like lying but I didn't say I hadn't eaten them either. My logic is easily explained by these facts:

1. If I told Mum I hadn't eaten them, she would have put more on my plate ...

AND...

2. If I did tell her then I would just get Grandad in trouble.

So, all in all, to 'fess up to Mum that I hadn't eaten the sprouts just seemed like a no win situation.

Grandad sat up straight with an innocent expression across his face. My grandad is AWESOME. I'm not sure my poor Nan will be so grateful when those extra evil balls of green yuckiness take effect later on, if they haven't already!

Other than the sprouts saga, the Christmas dinner was scrummy! Mum made the perfect trifle (luckily WITHOUT fruit this time) and Nan brought over her traditional Victoria Sponge filled with raspberry jam and LOADS of thick cream.

By the time I had finished eating, my clothes seem to have shrunk as they were SUPER tight and I felt like my belly was about to explode! Melly had fallen asleep in her high chair, with gravy around her face, and Grandad kept nodding off in his seat. Nan suggested we all go to the living room and in her words 'deflate on the sofa'. With the way I was feeling I didn't need telling twice.

After about an hour, when I felt a bit better and my clothes appeared to have grown back to their original size, me and Grandad set up the Zsphere 5 so we could play some of the games. Who knew that Nan and Grandad were epic gamers? We spent the whole afternoon playing Briks City. It's one of those games where you get to build and create items in your own virtual world. There are tasks to complete and battles to be fought... TOTALLY AWESOME.

Nan and Grandad went home about 5 o'clock. I was sad to see them go. As I was feeling a little glum about Christmas day being almost over, I asked mum if it was ok to call Elz to wish him Merry Christmas and to see what presents he got from Santa. He said that he had got a Zsphere 5 as well! That means we can play online with each other. Mum said that I should only play with the people I know in real life as you never really know if they really are who they say they are. Oh, and Mum said NEVER give out any details about yourself like your age, address or what school you go to because that can be really dangerous. There is a lot of good stuff about the internet and playing online but there are also a lot of dangers too which means I have to be really careful and sensible. Although saying that, the only one I really want to play with is Elz anyway so, one friend online for me is enough and he already knows everything about me so he wouldn't even have to ask.

Elz and I made a plan to play tomorrow which has taken the glumness away. Now I have something to look forward to even though the main day is almost over.

Once again, it's nearly time for me to sleep and with perfect timing, I am now writing on the last page of my awesome diary. It seems I had just enough room to let you know all about the most AMAZING Christmas EVER.

See you soon with more
EPIC adventures.
Merry Christmas!
Love from
Charlie Bottle

CPSIA information can be obtained
at www.ICGtesting.com
Printed in the USA
LVHW022127120922
728185LV00004B/102